EBONY OLSON

Black Mark's Resistance

Book 1: Black Mark Series

Sydney, Australia

EBANDMUSE PUBLICATIONS

Published 2019

Published by EbandMuse Publications

Sydney, Australia

ISBN: 978-0-6485000-1-8

Other Books Available by Ebony Olson
Hotel Series
Henderson
Cassidy
Holmes
Best Man

Black Mark Series
Black Mark's Resistance
Black Mark's Secret
Black Mark's Heart

Hierarch Series
Succumb

Standalones
Of Shadow and Light

Chapter One

Reaching the landing before the last flight of stairs, I paused to catch my breath. I preferred the stairs to the elevator, claiming it was for fitness, but in truth, I was extremely claustrophobic. Taking the deodorant out of my bag, I quickly gave myself a freshen up. My fine long black hair was pulled back in a tight ponytail, but I checked to make sure it was still presentable after seven flights of stairs.

The morning meeting with an upmarket clothing brand across town was still going. My boss, Stuart Shuman, had sent me back to entertain his next client until he could get back here. The client was the owner of Lynwood Corporation, the figurehead for bookings in the entertainment industry.

If you had the money, Lynwood offered the complete package for your event. They designed, developed and delivered everything from major public events, product launches, award shows, red carpet, the big fashion shows, gala dinners, concerts, corporate conferences, seminars and weddings for the rich and famous.

They would provide anything, from intimate acoustic acts to comedians, magicians, costumed tributes and everything in between- and I do mean everything. Lynwood agents worked with the client and took care of booking top-name entertainment. They organized the decor, sound and lighting. If you could think of a popular event in England in the last four years with headlining acts, more than likely, Lynwood had been the driving force behind it.

After reapplying my lip gloss and straightening my sensible black work dress, I took the last flight of stairs and plastered my smile into place. Walking through the glass doors into the reception area, I found two men sitting in the waiting area, looking at their watches unhappily.

"Mr. Rafal." I smiled walking toward them.

The dark-haired man stood instantly turning toward me. His hazel eyes scanned me from toe to head, his mouth frowning, his pupils dilating.

Ignoring the mixed look of disappointment and interest I held my hand out. "I'm Mora Ellis, Mr. Shuman's executive assistant. He's asked me to apologize for running late. He's caught up with another client currently, but should arrive shortly."

He shook my hand then pointedly looked at his watch. "I have somewhere else to be by one," he said, a faded Scottish accent evident.

"Then I will have Mr. Schuman's partner and our director of operations start the meeting. Mr. Shuman can join when he can," I assured. Stepping past the potential new client, I moved to the reception desk. "Melissa, can you ask Mr. Hark to join us immediately, please?"

"Yes, Miss Ellis." Melissa's thick Scottish accent outshone Mr. Rafal's.

Stepping back, I eyed Darius Rafal. He was tall, easily six-foot-four, or an inch or two more. I'd met him once, five years ago when I'd first moved to England. He hadn't changed at all. He was clean-shaven, late twenties, his dark hair was slightly too long for business, but suited him well, accentuating his strong jawline.

Everything about Mr. Rafal was tailored and precise. His navy suit matched perfectly with his tie. A black onyx tie pin caught my eye before his hands fidgeted with the matching onyx cuff links, stealing my focus.

When I lifted my topaz blue eyes to meet his hazel eyes, one of his eyebrows rose at my gumption. His blond male colleague smirked and stepped forward holding out his hand.

"I'm Warren Mann, Mr. Rafal's executive assistant. It's lovely to meet you, Mora." The London accent was crisper than most of my colleagues. "I love your accent. South African?"

"Australian."

Warren's blue eyes shone with humor as he shook my hand. He scanned my face, his eyes literally taking in the arch of my dark brows, the small bridge of my nose which my glasses always slipped down, my barely existent cheekbones, and the perfect Cupid's bow of my lips. I felt like he was memorizing what I looked like.

He was older, easily in his mid-thirties, clean cut and almost military in his presentation. While the suit was tailored, he wore a short-collared button-down which prevented him from wearing a tie. It also meant the small collar didn't come high enough to cover the dark bruising of teeth marks on his neck.

"Your girlfriend has a bad crossbite." I met his eyes evenly.

He returned my gaze, surprised at my openness. "If she were my girlfriend, I'd pay for the braces. Luckily, that's not the case."

"Lucky for her not to be your girlfriend, or for you not to have to pay for the braces?" I queried evenly. No judgment, just discerning the facts.

Warren smiled brightly. "Probably both. Your teeth would leave a perfect bruise."

"That they do." Looking past Warren to his boss, I smiled politely. "If you'll follow me," I requested politely. I turned toward the conference room.

The tall, dark-haired and blue-eyed Alex Hark was walking into the room as I approached from the reception area. He shook hands and introduced himself before turning to me and murmuring, "Catch me up."

"Standard marketing proposal. Mr. Rafal runs Lynwood Corporation. We want a piece of the pie."

Melissa came in with a pot of sencha green tea and sat it in front of the clients along with a specific brand of lemon shortbread. Stuart liked me to research prospective clients and know what they wanted. He called it good business, I called it stalking.

"Where in Scotland are you from?" Mr. Rafal picked up the teacup as he spoke to Melissa.

"Aberdeen. You?" She tucked a fiery strand of her hair behind her ear and batted her lashes.

"Inverness." Putting the tea to his lips, Rafal turned his shoulder away from her. He hadn't been flirting. Now, his body language told me that her flirtations annoyed him. He was shutting her down before she got the wrong idea.

"Did you go to the University of Highlands and Islands?" Melissa pushed on enthusiastically.

Swallowing his tea, Darius placed it down carefully before turning hard eyes on Melissa. Melissa dropped her eyes and stepped back in almost a gesture of submission. "I studied economics and international relations at the University of Saint Andrews. I got my MBA at the Imperial College of London."

Placing my hand on Melissa's shoulder gently, I interrupted his haunting glare. "Thank you, Melissa." Never lifting her eyes from the ground, Melissa quickly left the room. "Unnecessary," I stated factually when she shut the door.

"I'm sorry?" Darius Rafal lifted those hard eyes to meet mine.

Resisting the temptation to flinch, I leaned my hip on the table next to him. "Melissa was just welcoming and friendly towards a fellow Scotsman."

"I don't need a new friend." Darius kept his challenging eyes locked on mine.

"Well, you could use some manners," I huffed, standing straight.

"Mora," Alex breathed my name in warning.

Without acknowledging the warning, I walked to the door. "I'll leave you in Alex's capable hands." I had no patience for anyone who mistreated a woman.

"I believe Mr. Shuman instructed you to entertain me till he arrived, Miss Ellis," Darius Rafal spoke evenly before taking another sip of tea.

Glancing back as I opened the door, I noted Darius sat with his back to me, his assistant restraining the grin that was already lighting up his blue eyes. "You have rather large strong hands, Mr. Rafal. I'm sure since you don't need any new friends, that you are quite capable of entertaining yourself."

Bowing his head, Alex cursed. Darius turned his angry eyes to mine. Giving myself points for not flinching under that look, I winked at him and walked out. The moment I did, his assistant burst out laughing.

"I apologize, Mr. Rafal. Mora has no patience for people who think they are better than anyone else," Alex apologized as I shut the door.

"Are you suggesting I'm a snob, Mr. Hark?"

"I'm not suggesting it, Mr. Rafal. Now, if you turn to page two of the proposal in front of you..."

***

"Jesus, Mora, you are going to get yourself fired." Alex grabbed my elbow, yelling over the deep beat of the music. We were inside Jasper's nightclub, called JJ's, in Camden Town.

"Hey, you're here." Gifting Alex a mile and ignoring the comment, I handed him a shot from the tray I was carrying. "We're over here."

Keeping the tray over my head, I navigated my way through the crowd to the lounges where my best friend and her colleagues had planted themselves. It was already ten and Sophie, and her orchestra friends, had spent the first few hours of Friday night at the pub near their rehearsal hall.

"I mean it, Mora. Rafal made a comment to Stuart about your attitude. He then pointedly mentioned he was meeting with a competitor of ours this afternoon. Stuart must think you lost us the contract."

"Pfft! That ass was never going to give Horizons the contract. He gave us thirty minutes. He spent two hours with Elliptical, and an hour and a half with Objective before they even came to us. We were just time fill. Stuart knew that. Why do you think he didn't bother racing back for the meeting? We got the Sanderson contract, by the way."

Grinning, I passed out the shots, throwing back one before I dropped down into the lounge beside Sophie, my best friend. Flicking her golden curls over her shoulder, Sophie batted her lashes at Alex. She leaned forward to grab her shot, ensuring her extraordinary cleavage nearly fell out of her top.

"Yeah, Alex, relax. You know Mora knows what's going on with all of your clients. She'd never piss off a big client if there were any chance you could get them." Sophie winked at him and crossed her legs, the skirt she wore riding up higher on her thighs. "Now, bring your sexy ass over here and let me lick the salt off you."

"It's vodka, not tequila," Alex argued, sitting on my other side.

"Do I care?" Sophie threw back the shot anyway.

Alex and Sophie were banging each other. I knew about it, though no one else did, especially not Alex's girlfriend. Sophie was already well past tipsy. That meant her social filter went out the window three rounds of shots ago. How Alex's girlfriend hadn't caught on yet was beyond me. I guess she was too focused on the potential I was hooking up with her boyfriend to even suspect or notice any other woman.

That's what happens when another woman finds out you aren't in a monogamous relationship. They instantly suspect you of screwing every man you talk to. Because, when the guy everyone thinks is your sweetheart starts getting it on with another woman in your presence, and you don't bat an eyelash that obviously means you are also screwing around.

"Leila will be here soon, so cool it, Sophie," Alex warned.

"Why do you invite her out with us? She hates me and spends the entire night giving me daggers or trying to psychoanalyze my relationship with Jasper."

Alex patted my leg and kissed my cheek, giving me a sympathetic smile. So of course, that's precisely when Leila arrived. Her face went bright red with anger, and I knew she was getting ready to start calling me several unsavory names again. Rolling my eyes, I grabbed Alex's chin and kissed him. It was closed mouth and awkward as hell, but I pressed my lips to his for several seconds before pulling away and standing. My eyes all for Leila. "Now call me all the names you want."

Alex was still sitting shocked by my kiss. He didn't even realize Leila was there till I'd walked away and Leila screeched like a cockatoo. "I knew it!"

Sophie was laughing so hard she tipped sideways on the lounge and nearly fell off. One of her friends caught her, and they laughed together. At the bar I signaled the barman for another round.

"Celebrating tonight, Mora?" Winston rolled up the white sleeves of his shirt, which only made the dark flesh underneath look darker.

"Hell, yes. I scored big today."

Winston grinned his pearly whites at me. "One more round, then I'm cutting you ladies off before Sophie gets herself in trouble. After this, single drinks only. Understood?"

"Fine! Punish me for the hot girl's shortcomings," I teased. Winston knew I could handle my alcohol better than Sophie. He didn't want to be cleaning up her puke in another hour.

"And what big score did you make today?" A deep voice whispered in my ear.

I turned to find Warren Mann grinning at me. The top two buttons of his shirt were undone, the jacket was gone and his eyes were bright and glassy. He'd had a few drinks already and was apparently there to relax. He reached out and tucked my hair behind my ear.

"I like your hair out. You look your age now."

Young is what he was saying, but then he was at least ten years my senior. I liked Warren. He was friendly, flirty, and just gave off those good vibes. He was looking over the little black dress that I was wearing, but his eyes paused for a moment longer than appropriate on the scoop neck, and how the material clung around my breasts.

"Not your boss, that's for sure." Smirking, I used my finger under his chin to lift his eyes back to mine. "You winding down after a long day?"

Warren held up a glass of scotch and ice. "Sure am. Want to help me?"

"Sure. Come join us."

Winston slid a second glass in front of Warren. "Thanks." Warren took the glass. "I'll just go grab my jacket."

Nodding acknowledgment, I watched the very buff Mr. Mann walk off into the crowd. "Last round, Mora," Winston reminded me as he slid another tray of shots in front of me.

Crossing my heart, I blew him a kiss. Giving me another one of his disarming smiles, Winston waved me off. Balancing the tray above my head like I still worked the bar to get through the crowd, I swerved my way over to the quiet corner we nabbed. When I put the tray down, the group all grabbed a shot. We saluted each other before throwing them back. I threw back my own shot while standing, then set it on the low table.

"There you are," Warren called behind me.

Standing straight, I turned around still filled with the success of my day. The smile disappeared when I saw my failure standing with Warren. Darius Rafal was gorgeous in daylight; darkness didn't detract from it. He now had a five o'clock shadow that made him look more rugged. It also made some primal sexual beast inside me start rolling around and purring. I was saved from actually purring out loud by Alex.

"What the hell is with you today, Mora? Are you PMSing or something?" Alex growled. He pushed past me to grab his jacket from the lounge. The way I was reacting to Darius Rafal made ovulating the more likely theory. Alex shook his head angrily. "You owe me big time. I have to go do damage control."

Sophie latched onto Alex's arm. "Leave the bitch. Stay. You deserve to relax. I can make it happen." Sophie licked her lips suggestively.

Alex hesitated, considering the option. He closed his eyes and shook his head. "Shit, you women are going to put me in an early grave." Pulling out of Sophie's drunken hold, Alex turned to leave. He saw Darius and Warren watching. He glanced back to me, annoyance clear on his face before he laughed and looked at Darius. "Be careful. This lot look like angels, but they are deadly."

"Love you too, Alex." I smiled.

Alex gave me a half smile over his shoulder, waved and disappeared into the crowd. Picking up my bottle of water, I took a long drink and plastered a smile on my face.

"Mora, you going to introduce us?" Sophie pointed to Warren and Darius.

"This is Warren Mann, he works at Lynwood, and that asshole is his boss."

Yeah, maybe Alex might have been right. I was definitely in a shit-stirring mood today. Though, it started with being in the room with Darius and his broad shoulders that would be great to sink my teeth and nails into. Maybe he'd thrown my hormones out of whack.

"Are you always so straight forward with all strangers?" Darius grumbled before giving his smirking assistant a dark look.

"With everyone."

"What are you doing with everyone?" A deep voice queried as strong hands wrapped around my waist and pulled me tight against a hard body.

Recognizing Jasper instantly, I grinned. Thank god I'd been drinking to handle this moment. "Being my usual charming self."

Darius's face shut down the moment Jasper touched me. Warren also seemed to sober up and stood straighter. Jasper turned my face to my shoulder and kissed my mouth tenderly. "I've missed you. Let's go back to my office." He nuzzled my neck before biting my shoulder hard enough to bruise.

Biting my lip, I let my head hang back as his hands moved lower to arrest my hips. Jasper lifted his mouth to my ear. "I want to eat that sweet cunt of yours while you wrap that beautiful mouth around my hard cock."

I groaned. To say I was randy after two weeks without was an understatement. Jasper turned me to face him, his green irises were barely visible by how large his pupils were. He wasn't model good-looking, but he had confidence and charisma that was far more appealing. He was a successful nightclub owner, so women weren't in short supply for him, and even in his early thirties, his body under those clothes was worth getting on your knees to worship.

Jasper kissed me hard, his fingers threading into my long black hair. When he pulled back, he licked over my lips. "My office, now."

He took my hand and pulled me after him through the crowd. Glancing back over my shoulder, I waved goodbye to Darius Rafal and Warren Mann, some of my joy dissipating. They'd surely be gone by the time I made my way back out to the club. Considering they didn't want our business, I'd probably never see them again.

Chapter Two

"What is that horrible noise?" Jasper groaned hiding beneath his pillow next to me.

"My phone," I growled, rolling over to collect it from the bedside table. "Hello?" I gave myself points for sounding wide awake. Peering at the clock, I saw the first number was seven and groaned internally.

"Miss Ellis, I was hoping we could have breakfast this morning," a mild Scottish accent came through the phone.

"Who is this?" Checking the screen, I saw it was a private number.

"Darius Rafal. I'll meet you at Lucina's in an hour."

"What..." The dial tone came through the earpiece. "Son of a bitch," I grumbled sitting up in bed. "I have to go."

"Since when does Stuart call you into work on a Saturday?" Jasper turned his face halfway to peer out at me from under his pillow.

"Stuart is probably still passed out after his celebrations last night." Throwing back the sheet, I climbed out of Jasper's bed. "That was a client. I need to meet them in an hour."

"Come back afterwards? I need some more sleep, but I'd like to spend the afternoon with you."

"Sure." I shut the bathroom door with a smile. Jasper was my weekends. During the week, I lived and breathed work, but the weekends were my time. Remembering why I was out of bed so early, I frowned. Why was I rushing off to meet with Darius Rafal just because he called? Because he hung up before you could tell him where he could stick his meeting. Oh, well. At least I'd get a delicious breakfast out of it.

I arrived at Lucina's five minutes before the hour was up. Darius Rafal was already there sipping his tea and watching me approach. He wore a green polo shirt and chinos with what looked to be volleys, but a much more expensive version. This was Darius in casual mode. He looked like he was on his way to the golf club. He was pointedly looking at his watch as Darius set down the tea.

"Well, that's an improvement on yesterday." Biting back the retort on my tongue because I could see the jerk waiting for it, I slipped into the chair opposite him without a word. He nodded as if approving. "Coffee?"

"I don't drink coffee, thank you." Leaning forward I caught the eye of Jackie, who regularly worked Saturday mornings and waved. She smiled, signalled she knew I was there and walked off into the kitchen. "What can I do for you so early on a Saturday, Mr. Rafal?"

"Explain yesterday to me."

"Excuse me?" I asked utterly confused.

"You were late. I've been told you are never late. You were rude. I was informed you are very well-mannered. You walked away from the deal leaving someone who knew nothing about it to try and garner my interest. I'd like you to explain why you behaved the exact opposite to the way you do for every other client and your employer." He picked up his tea and took another sip.

Jackie put a glass full of green liquid in front of me. "Usual, Mora?"

"Yes please, Jackie."

"And you sir?" Jackie eyed Darius like I would a cheesecake.

"The big breakfast please." Darius handed his menu to Jackie and turned his attention to my drink. "What is that?"

"Refreshing green goodness." Taking a large sip, I moaned as the refreshing taste of mint, lime and apple tantalized my taste buds.

"Also known as?" Darius pushed.

"I don't know. Lots of fruit and herbs that wake me up after a late night."

"I wouldn't call ten late."

"I didn't get to bed until one, sleep was even later."

"You and your friends hit the shots hard last night. Is that normal practice for you?"

Raising a brow as I took another drink, pointedly ignoring his question. Darius Rafal watched me, his eyes turning hard as I drank in silence. "I should warn you, Miss Ellis. I am used to having my questions answered immediately upon asking."

"If you sign my paychecks, you get to boss me around, make demands, and ask me questions that are relevant to the job. As nobody in my life, you are entitled to none of the above."

Darius sat back, fingers of both hands tapping on his teacup. "I am a potential client and—"

Frustrated, I put the glass down. "No, you're not. You were never going to give the contract to us. Stop bullshitting me. You've obviously been told my reputation, so here's one you missed. I'm very forward and factual. Some people take my straight down the line attitude as being abrupt and forceful, but it's simply that I am too busy to put up with shit. So cut the shit, Mr. Rafal. What do you want?"

Darius's eyes flared open, pupils dilating and one of his gorgeous brows kinked. "Is that why you were so ill-mannered yesterday? Because you were sure I was wasting your time?"

"Weren't you?" I lifted a brow. "You spent an hour and a half with Objective in the morning, and two hours with Elliptical in the afternoon. You gave us thirty minutes. We were fill-in-time. Horizon is small fry compared to Elliptical and Objective. So yes, Mr. Rafal, you were wasting my time. You are giving the contract to Elliptical. You and I know it."

Jackie slid two plates onto the table, her brows raised at the tension between us. "Can I get you anything else?"

"No, thank you." Gifting her a curteous smile, Darius waited till Jackie was well out of earshot. "You are right. My being there about the contract was pretence yesterday. I was there to meet you."

Pausing in picking up my cutlery, I watched Darius and sighed shaking my head. "No."

"No?" Darius lifted a brow, and a smile filling his eyes. "You don't even know what my real reason to be there was."

"You were either there to offer me a job or date me. Since you don't date, it's the job. For which my answer is no."

"You can read me that easily?" The beginnings of a real smile started on his face. Our eyes locked on each other as we sat silently for several breaths.

"Look, normally I would have gotten up and left by now, but this is my favorite place to eat and I'm starving. So, if you don't mind, I'll finish my breakfast first."

Darius sat back crossing his strong arms across his broad chest. "Why such a stern no to working for me?"

Swallowing my mouthful, I wiped my mouth with a napkin. "You have an executive assistant already, and he's damn good at his job. Whatever you are offering me isn't going to be as good as I've got now."

Darius watched me eat for a full minute before he picked up his knife and fork and started dividing the food on his plate. "You weren't kidding about being forward, were you?"

There was no point responding. I ate my breakfast silently. Darius started eating, watching me with curiosity. I finished eating before him, finished my juice and went to stand. "Thanks for breakfast and nice meeting you."

Darius put out his hand, catching my elbow to stop me sliding out of the seat. "Wait. Warren needs an assistant; his workload is too high to do by himself. I also need a personal assistant. My offer is for you to be my personal assistant. You will have your role split between my personal duties and assisting Warren." Darius let go of my elbow as I settled back into the seat. "I know what you earn at Horizon. You will be paid more, almost a fifty per cent raise actually because your workday won't stop when you get home."

When I opened my mouth to object, Darius gave me a level look and kept talking. "Your current living arrangements won't be an issue either. Warren and two other staff live with me. There is a room currently empty. I will have it furnished for you ready to move in, which I will expect within the fortnight."

"How did you know my living arrangements?"

Finally, Darius smiled. It took him from ruggedly good-looking to downright handsome. "You are not the only person who did their research before we met, Miss Ellis. The only surprise was your attitude yesterday, which contravened all reports of your professionalism, and your boyfriend at the club last night."

"My attitude yesterday was well deserved for the way you treated Melissa, Mr. Rafal. As for Jasper, I think boyfriend may be too strong a word."

Darius's smile faded, his eyes growing darker by the second. "He bit you while pointedly looking at me, Miss Ellis. He was letting me know you belong to him. That is definitely the behavior of a boyfriend."

Dropping my eyes to the table, I thought hard about my words. When I lifted them, Darius's darkness seemed to dissolve. "Jasper doesn't want commitment, and with my work ethic that works for both of us right now."

"His seeing other women doesn't bother you?" Darius assessed me.

"I'm twenty-two and work twelve hour days during the week. I'm happy to have a regular guy to relieve my tension with every Friday and Saturday. Where he relieves himself any other day is none of my business."

Darius's Adam's apple bob as he swallowed hard. "I hope you are taking precautions for the sake of your health then."

"Jasper is very careful. He doesn't need some woman getting knocked up on purpose and trying to get child support out of him. He takes the precautions to protect himself and I take the ones to protect me. How about you Mr. Rafal? Do you take precautions with your parade of lovers?"

That smile returned to his gorgeous face. "I can't remember the last time I came anywhere but in a woman's throat."

"You prefer oral?" I asked curiously, trying not to seem interested.

Darius lent forward. "My preferences are different."

"Is that why you regularly have married couples over to your place till late in the evening?"

Darius's eyes popped. "How the hell do you know about that?"

Suppressing the smile of victory, I stood. "I'll need to think about your offer. When do you want your answer?"

Darius sat back, still shocked by my knowledge of his personal life. I can understand why. He worked very hard to keep his personal life out of the media. He'd not been seen with a woman on his arm since he left college. "I want your answer now, Miss Ellis."

I shook my head. "I'm not spontaneous like that."

Darius stood, his body so close I could feel the heat from it. "On the spot decisions would be part of your job description, Miss Ellis. Make this one now or forfeit the offer."

I swallowed at his closeness. "I make well-informed decisions, I don't just jump."

"Very well. Firstly, there are very few women in my company, and you will not be permitted to fraternize with any of your co-workers. Since you will be living with me, you will need to sign a non-disclosure agreement. You will not bring any lovers back to my place. You will occasionally need to travel with me and weekend work will happen time-to-time, as well. I expect you will put your job above your social life, and there is no consumption of alcohol allowed during work hours. Anything else you need to know?"

He didn't move away and I stood staring at the small scar to the left of his larynx, thoughts rushing through my head at high speed. All the possible benefits and downfalls of working for Darius Rafal. "Study leave?"

His intake of breath sucked air across the top of my head. "You wish to return to studying?" His voice was even, no judgment.

"Not return, complete. I've never stopped." I lifted my eyes to meet his now. "I'm doing the extended project in my Master of Philosophy in Music Studies."

Darius frowned. "You are a music major?"

"I've nearly finished my project and dissertation, so it won't take up too much of my time. I just couldn't take a job that didn't allow me the time to finish this qualification."

Darius looked down between our two bodies. I was conscious of the scoop neck top I wore and how his height and proximity gave him a perfect view, but I didn't fidget. "Where are you doing your degree?"

"Cambridge."

Darius's brows jumped, his hazel eyes bored into mine. "Take the job, Mora. Working for me will open doors everywhere for you, no matter what future you plan."

***

"It cannot be true." Alex rested his butt on my desk and looked down at me with hurt eyes. "Stuart just told me you handed in your resignation this morning. Two weeks' notice given and you don't even tell your bestie."

I ignored him and kept typing the memo I was working on.

Alex dropped the hurt act and crouched down to create a false sense of privacy. "You left Friday celebrating you'd nearly singlehandedly closed that Sanderson deal, and today you give your notice. What happened over the weekend, Mora?"

"I was offered a better opportunity elsewhere," I answered still typing.

"Where?"

"Lynwood."

Alex's jaw fell open. "Who did you blow to get that role?"

"Hey!" I glared at Alex. "I was hired on my professional skills, asshole."

"I'm not kidding, Mora. I saw them at the club on Friday night. Jasper said you were good, but I didn't think that would get you a job at one of the most successful companies in the northern hemisphere."

"I'm not kidding either. I did not blow, have sex, or any type of sexual conduct with either Rafal or his assistant to get the job. I went home with Jasper, as usual."

"Then how did this happen?" Alex asked, outraged.

I looked at Alex exasperated. "Could you temper your attitude a little? You sound like I'm pregnant by a Columbian drug lord." Pressing print on the document, I turned to face Alex. "He called me Saturday morning and asked to meet me. Then he offered me the job. Apparently, Friday was my interview."

Alex raised an eyebrow. "Jeez, they must have some interesting standards over there. I'm pretty sure you less-than-subtly hinted your new boss was an asshole at that meeting."

"I called him one to his face at the club. Speaking of which, did you smooth things over with Leila?"

Alex blew out a breath. "I don't know why she is so hung up on her jealousy of you."

"Yeah, me neither," I replied, annoyed. From the moment Alex introduced us, Leila took issue with me. It prevented any chance of us liking each other.

"So, I guess you'll be moving out of the loft?" Alex quirked a brow at me. "Where are you going to live?"

Part of me was hesitant to reveal that truth. Only a handful of people knew I lived here at work. The loft access was from out the back, and was a studio apartment. It was used for storage till Alex cleaned it out for me to sleep there, with Stuart's permission, of course. I liked the coziness of the space, plus, it was my own space. No CEO mother and no irritated bachelor father.

Alex looked at his shoes. "You going to be okay out there in the big bad world by yourself, Mora?"

I smiled and touched his cheek gently. "It's time I found out, Alex. Thank you for taking care of me these last few years. You've been a good big brother. You should tell Leila the truth about us, it will put her at ease."

"If I tell Leila we share a father, I have to tell her who my father is. We both took our mothers' surnames so no one would associate us with him. Leila wants money enough to push for marriage as soon as she knows about Marshall."

That Alex and I were both the illegitimate offspring of a wealthy and powerful London businessman was such a well-kept secret, that only our respective mothers, our father, his lawyer and his accountant knew the truth.

Alex was nearly ten years older than me. His mother had a relationship with our father. They broke up when she found out she was pregnant and she married Alex's stepdad. Our father organized child support to be paid and also paid for Alex's schooling. Pretty much the same deal he set up with my mother when she informed him I existed.

My story differed from Alex's somewhat. My mother was a grad student interning at my father's company when they had an affair. She graduated, packed up and moved home to Australia, only to find her boss had sent her home with a present to always remember him by.

Alex and I were introduced shortly after I arrived in London, at a very private family dinner. Marshall Blake, our father, at least took interest in Alex growing up, taking time to watch his football games and graduation from college. Alex was delighted to find out he had a baby sister and took to the role of doting big brother happily.

Alex stood up. "Give me a heads up next time. You making spontaneous life-changing decisions is like a marker for the apocalypse."

"Sure." As I started walking away I looked back over my shoulder. "Heads up, Sophie has decided she wants something permanent and is going to give you an ultimatum to choose between her and Leila."

Alex's face lost all its color. With a wink, I turned the corner for the photocopier.

Chapter Three

The elevator doors opened. Opening my eyes, I rushed forward, drawing in a deep breath, resisting the urge to drop to the ground and pass out. I was on the top floor of Lynwood enterprises in Clerken Well. If the receptionist four flights below was curious about the two bags of luggage, and aqua blue cello case I pulled behind me, or the box under my arm, she hid it well.

I lugged my belongings after me down the wide slate-grey corridor lined with artwork. There were two large desks set on either side at the far end of the passage before the large ebony doors of Darius Rafal's office.

Warren stepped out of one of those doors opened as I approached, shutting the door behind him. He looked up at me, smiled and placed his tablet and stylus on the desk to his right.

"Welcome aboard, Mora." Coming forward, Warren relieved me of the box I carried. He took the handle of the large case, which had the cabin bag tied neatly on top, and a wheelie cello case held together with an occy strap to pull along with it. "I'll have someone collect the rest of your belongings later."

"This is it."

Warren's smile faded as he set my luggage out of the way. "This is everything you own?"

"Yes."

Today Warren wore a classic button-down with his suit. He adjusted his tie in discomfort. "Okay. Well, this is your desk." He indicated the desk opposite where he'd placed his tablet. "Your computer is ready to go. Your tablet and work mobile are set up with the programs we use for communication and time management.”

Stepping behind the desk, Warren opened the drawer on the return, pulling out the aforementioned items and an envelope. “Your passwords are in here, along with keys to the house and office, and a passkey for the elevator.”

Warren dropped the envelope in the drawer as I put my handbag down and removed my mid-season jacket, hanging it over the back of the chair.

“What are you wearing?” Warren looked me over, shaking his head.

Peering at my grey slacks and black blouse, I frowned. I couldn’t see anything wrong with it. I looked professional and well presented.

Warren shook his head. “You are female. Dresses or skirt and blouse. No pants unless you are going to the gym. Grab a skirt out of your bag and get changed. The toilet is by the elevator.” Warren walked to his desk.

My jaw dropped open. “This isn’t the fifties. Women wear slacks.”

“Not in this company they don’t.”

“I couldn’t exactly trudge across London with all my luggage in a skirt and look decent by the end of it.”

Warren sat at his desk and sighed. “Fair enough, but your luggage will be taken care of now, so grab a skirt and go change, Mora. When you get back, I’ll introduce you to the head of security and other relevant staff.” Warren turned back to his computer without another word.

Taking a deep breath to keep my temper, I untied my suitcases and dug out a black flared skirt and a pair of heels. That’s the other reason I wore slacks; so I could wear comfortable flats. I closed my suitcase and stood up just as the ebony doors opened and Darius stalked out. “Is she here yet?” he asked looking at Warren.

Warren pointed to me. Turning toward me, Darius looked me over, his nostrils flaring when he saw my slacks. He opened his mouth, but I held up the skirt.

"Just going to change. Didn't want to flash anyone my lace panties while traipsing over town, boss."

Darius's eyes widened slightly at the mention of my underwear then he closed them, clearly counting to ten in his head. When his eyes opened, he looked somewhat calmer. "Welcome to Lynwood, Miss Ellis. Warren will get you settled in, and we will meet later to get you started."

When I nodded, Darius turned to Warren and started telling him where he was going while I walked down the corridor to the bathroom.

Swinging open the door, I blinked at the opulence. It was a bit over the top for a bathroom, especially in an office building with very few females. There was a plush stool in front of a mirror that was set up for the application of makeup. An array of mini perfume bottles were lined up on the counter, all of which were out of my price range. There was a shower as well as the toilet and a pile of fluffy lavender scented towels.

Shaking the confusion of the scene out of my head, I quickly changed my pants and shoes and walked back out to the office. Darius was adjusting his cuff links while he waited in front of the elevator. "I gather the bathroom was to your liking?"

He didn't look at me, just kept tidying himself. Checking back over my shoulder at the bathroom, I was concerned he'd set that up just for me.

"A bit opulent for me." He looked at me then, surprise in his eyes. I shrugged. "I'm a practical girl and not very materialistic. The heated floors are nice though, that's a luxury I'll never say no to." With a smile, I started back to my desk.

Packing my clothes away, I sank into my very expensive, but supportive desk chair. Warren was on the phone, so I took out the envelope and logged into my brand new computer and opened my email. There was one from Warren waiting.

I'm going to be twenty minutes. D needs his dry-cleaning picked up. Take your tablet and phone. I'll have a car waiting for you by the time you get downstairs. See you when you get back.

Grabbing the phone and tablet, I stuffed them into my handbag and collected my key pass, waving to Warren as I walked out. He acknowledged me and kept talking. I was stepping toward the fire exit when the elevator opened. A tall, well-built blond man in his late twenties stepped out. His blue eyes took me in in one glance, a smile slipping into place.

"Miss Ellis, I was just coming to see you. Are you heading out already?"

"Yes, I have an errand to run," I answered stepping toward the fire exit.

He held the elevator door, brows drawn in as he watched me. "I'll ride down with you."

"I prefer to take the stairs." Pushing open the door, I was surprised when his big hand caught the door as he followed me into the stairwell.

"Then I'll walk down with you." He handed me a card in a plastic case with an alligator clip. "I'm Zander Mann, head of security. That's your identification. You'll need to wear it inside the building. It will get you inside the staff gates and to all our floors in the building."

Frowning, I took out the other key pass I'd been given. "What is this one for then?"

Zander looked at the card and smiled. "That is for the front gate at the house."

"Oh." Slipping it back in my purse, I started down the stairs. The photo on the ID card was from this morning. Thank god I'd applied a little makeup before coming in. I clipped it onto my waistband. "You have the same surname as Warren?"

"Yes. We're brothers," Zander smiled as we approached the ground floor. "I went to college with Darius and introduced them. We've been good friends since." Pulling open the ground floor door, he held it for me to pass. I was surprised when he kept walking with me.

"So you live at the house also?"

His smile grew. "Yes, Miss Ellis."

"Please call me Mora."

"As you like, Mora." Zander walked me out and directed me to a waiting town car and the driver. "Clark, I believe this is your passenger."

Clark, the driver, was my age, his brown eyes looking me over as he bobbed his head and opened the back door. I cringed at the small quarters of the back seat. Unfortunately, Zander saw it.

"Clark, after today, when you need to drive Miss Ellis, you'll take the Rolls Royce," Zander instructed.

"Yes, Mr. Mann."

Zander grabbed the door and made a hand gesture, so Clark slid in behind the driver's seat. I met Zander's kind blue eyes. "We will take care of you here, Mora. You don't like confined spaces, we will give you as much space as you need."

"Thank you, Zander." I touched his upper arm. "Do me a favor?" He nodded. "If he's filled my room with frilly pink florals and perfumed stuff, can you maybe organize it to be gone before I get home. He may be offended if I prefer to sleep on the lounge otherwise."

Zander gave me a humored smirk. "You need not worry. Steffen is over the moon about having a woman in the house, but we have kept him restrained in the decorating."

"Steffen?"

"You will meet him tonight, but right now," Zander looked at his watch, "you need to get moving."

I smiled and dropped into the back seat, careful to tuck my legs so I didn't flash Zander. After he closed the door, the car instantly pulled out into traffic.

"Just the dry cleaner's, Miss Ellis?"

A phone pinged several times. After waiting for Clark to answer his phone, I realized it was coming from my bag. I pulled out my new work phone.

While you are out...

"That's where we'll start, Clark." I sighed looking at the list Warren sent me.

***

Thankfully, Clark knew precisely where to go for each job. I was in and out as quick as I could be. After collecting the dry-cleaning, I was sent to collect Darius's new suit from the tailor. He insisted on taking my measurements while I was there. I bit my tongue with the hands moving to wrap the tape around my chest, but when the tailor's hand went up my skirt to measure my inseam, I ended that party.

Then it was a stop for Darius's new shoes from a boutique shoemaker who insisted on me trying on a pair of his heels. The shoes were cute but not to my taste or budget. More disturbing was the way the guy touched my feet. Definitely a foot fetishist.

The last stop was the jeweler for a new pair of cuff links to go with his new suit. I was asked if there was anything I wanted to try while the jeweler went out the back to get the package. There was nothing in this place within range of my budget. I thought the sales assistant was going to burst into tears when I declined to even look.

I quickly glanced at the case in front of me, saw a beautiful pair of topaz and diamond earrings and asked how much they were. That resulted in her shoving the matching topaz ring on my ring finger and brandishing the matching bracelet and necklace, by which time I was regretting being nice.

Nearly two hours past by the time I finished everything on the list. Shoving open the fire door on the top floor, thanking Darius inwardly that he owned a four-story, converted industrial building, I walked quickly to my desk. Zander was there talking to Warren giving me a big smile as I approached.

"How did you go?"

"Got everything on the list and a few extras."

Checking his watch, Warren lifted his eyebrows. "I thought you'd be longer. What extras?"

Dropping my handbag behind my desk, I threw the suits over my chair and walked to his side of the office with one of the large bags I was carrying. "The jeweler is across the road from a wonderful French patisserie that makes the most delicious lemon tarts. I picked some up to serve for morning tea. A little birdie also told me you are a sucker for a good macaroon, so I got you a sampler box." I placed the box down in front of Warren as I checked the time. "Is he back yet?"

"Yes," Warren answered, opening the box of macaroons and taking a deep breath. A smile lighting his face up.

"Should I see if he wants morning tea?" I asked walking back to my desk and into the small kitchenette past it.

Warren stood. "Leave the tarts, grab the other stuff, and I'll show you how this works."

Placing the tarts in the fridge, I grabbed up the suits and the other bag and followed Warren to a side door behind his desk.

Warren put his finger to his lips. "If you know he's not in the office or you need to interrupt him, you can walk in the main doors. All other times, it's this door. This will take us into the back end of his office without interrupting any meeting or phone call he may be having. There are also times when he is so bogged down that he will not want to be disturbed. If you go in this way and he ignores you, you leave him be. If he talks to you, it's fine to enter the office area. Understood?"

When I nodded, Warren pushed open the door and held it while I followed him into the tight corridor, leading the way around the office. Through the glass wall and sheer curtain, I could see Darius reading a report on his screen and adding comments. His jacket was off, his tie gone and his top button undone. He wore glasses and looked damn sexy with that focused look on his face.

Reaching the end of the glassed hallway, we were in a small wardrobe. A pair of leather dress shoes, two suits—one black, one grey—and ties. Off the closet was an open bathroom with a rainmaker shower head, toilet, and vanity. I would have to be sure to check he wasn't using the bathroom before coming in this way or I would see a whole lot more of my boss than needed. I went to ask that question, but Warren put his finger to my lips, gestured to the stuff I held, and then the wardrobe. Without another word he walked back out the way he came in.

With a sigh, I put down the bag and started hanging up the suits. Removing the shoes from the box, I set them neatly on the shoe rack, then opened a drawer to deposit the cuff links alongside a variety of others. Once done, I put the shoebox back in the bag and went to leave.

"Miss Ellis?" Darius called.

I stepped hesitantly forward, wary that I'd screwed up. Darius kept his eyes on the screen as I moved around the corner and into the office. "Yes, sir."

"Don't call me that, I'm not knighted. Here you can call me Darius or boss. In public it's Mr. Rafal."

"Yes, boss."

"You are claustrophobic?"

"Yes, boss," I answered clearly, resisting the urge to hunch in shame. That's probably why Zander was up here when I got back.

"Severe?"

"Depends on the situation. I survived the elevator this morning."

"Did something happen to cause it?"

"Yes, boss." I didn't expand on it. My childhood wasn't his business.

Darius stopped what he was doing and turned to look at me, removing his glasses as he did. "Did you ever go to counseling for it?" he asked gently, carefully.

My shoulders rolled forward before I could stop them. "No." Taking a breath, I rolled my damn shoulders back. "It's morning tea time. I picked up some delicious tarts while I was out if you would like one?"

"That sounds good. Thank you."

Giving Darius a single nod, I walked toward the ebony office doors. I could feel his eyes on me with every step. As I stepped out the door, I dared to turn my head and met those hazel eyes. He blinked, and they hardened before he slipped his glasses back on and turned back to his screen. The second before that—well, I'm sure I was wrong.

In the kitchen, I dumped the bags in the rubbish and made Darius his sencha tea, put the tarts on plates surrounded by a small amount of sliced fruit, and made Warren and I tea. "That for the boss?" Warren spoke behind me.

"One is, the others are ours."

"I'll take it in. I've got to discuss tonight with him."

Placing two of the plates and their teas on the serving tray, I handed it to him with a smile.

"Thanks. I've sent you instructions on how to access our working files. I need you to look over a report for me for errors, and then we should get that induction over with. You need to meet the event planning team, logistics, and the service coordination team. After that, I'll take you across the road to the Design House and introduce you to the team there." Warren started to walk away.

"What about the concept team?" There would be a team in place for initial meetings and coming up with any concepts like themes and layouts.

Warren smiled at me. "You were just in his office." Waiting for my brows to rise, Warren then sobered as he headed for the office doors. "Do you have any plans tonight?"

"I have a class at eight."

Warren stopped and looked back at me. "For college?"

"No, it's a fitness class." When Warren frowned, I smiled. "Guess your researcher missed that as well?"

"Obviously."

My smile grew. "That means you only checked me out for a week before we met. I hadn't seen Jasper for two weeks and missed classes to work back on a project."

"Is that your way of telling me we are in for some surprises?" Warren grumbled. I shrugged. Warren shook his head in dismay. "Put the address of your gym in the contacts so I can find you if I need you," he instructed and pushed through the ebony doors.

***

Darius Rafal's apartment was in Kensington, tucked between Hyde Park and Holland Park. It was an exquisite property arranged over the top two floors of an imposing gated development.

"It's four bedrooms, all with en-suites. There are two reception rooms, an eat-in kitchen, home office, media room, a massage room and a separate studio flat with shower room for Steffen, the butler, and chef," Clark informed me as he pulled up out front.

As instructed, Clark now drove a Rolls Royce Ghost with the extended wheelbase, giving me a feeling of more room in the back. The apartment was situated within one of Kensington's most desired and exclusive areas which offer manicured communal gardens.

"There's a communal swimming pool and twenty-four-hour concierge. You should be quite comfortable here," Clark smiled opening my door. "Your key pass will get you inside, Miss Ellis, then up to the fourth floor. Steffen will be there to show you around."

"Thank you, Clark." I smiled sliding out of the car.

Swiping my key pass at the gate, I then repeated the process at the front door. The door buzzed open and let me in. Taking the stairs up, there was a man easily in his fifties waiting at the door for me. His face cracked in a smile when he saw me.

"Miss Ellis. Welcome home." He opened the double doors and stepped into the wide foyer holding the door for me. "It's lovely to finally have a female presence in the house."

"You say that now. Just wait till my period kicks in." I expected Steffen to flinch, he didn't.

"I have three grown daughters, Miss Ellis. All fell into the same cycle. I assure you, I've seen perfect angels turn into the most hellish beasts." He glanced at me, a sparkle in his eyes. I realized I'd misjudged his age by at least ten years. He was sixty-something, but sprightly and still full of youth. "Any attempts to shock an old English gentleman will also fail. I'm quite well rounded in my education."

"I wouldn't expect anything else from one of Mr. Rafal's employees." I smiled.

Steffen smiled back and gestured for me to follow him. The luxury was evident immediately with the double height ceilings, and touchscreen pads throughout which control the entertainment, lighting and heating system. At the fork, he stopped and pointed to the right.

"Kitchen is the first door on the left. The double doors straight ahead are the master's suite. You will only enter there upon his request."

The way he phrased that made me think my job description would need rewriting if that ever happened.

Moving to the left, we entered a large reception area open through to the fifth floor and the ceiling. There was a large sitting area immediately ahead, a large dining table to the rear of the room, a mini grand piano huddled in the far corner and a large fireplace set within a wall to split the room and hide a smaller sitting area. The colors were stone, creams, black, and timber.

Steffen walked through the room to the opposite side. There was a door in the wall leading into a foyer, above which rose a flight of stairs. "Through there are the library and the office. Your room is this way." Walking to the base of the stairs, Steffen climbed with impressive agility.

I followed him up, admiring the iron banister wrought of twisted metal vines. From the top of the stairs, I could look over the entire reception area. On the far side, I saw an identical flight of stairs above the door to the foyer and kitchen. At the top of those stairs was a landing with a lounge.

On this side, there was a door and a closet. Opening the door, Steffen led me into my room. Immediately upon the left of the entry was the cream marble en-suite, consisting of a large bathtub, shower, and a gorgeous mirrored vanity.

The bedroom had polished timber floors, a four-door wardrobe along one wall, a large white framed bed with white satin and black fake fur quilt cover, two bedside tables, and a chest at the end of the bed. Beyond the bed were double doors leading onto the wrap-around terrace. My cello stood in the corner on its stand, the music stand already set up next to it. To say the apartment was beautiful would be an understatement.

"You are the only person situated on this side of the apartment. It should be quite peaceful for you."

"It's lovely." I grinned, barely able to believe how stunningly beautiful it was. Walking to the terrace doors, I looked out. The view was over the rooftops toward Hyde Park. It was breathtaking.

"I have taken the liberty to unpack your belongings and put them away for you." Steffen tapped the wardrobe door.

Slightly horrified at the thought of him unpacking my underwear, not to mention, other more personal items, I blushed.

Steffen laughed. "As I explained downstairs, miss, I am hard to shock. I have put your diary and your toy in your bedside table on the far side from the door." Biting my lip, I felt myself blush harder. This seemed to encourage Steffen.

"Really, miss, in this day and age, I believe a vibrator is a standard female possession." He opened the wardrobe door and pulled out my Eeyore pillow pet, holding it up. "This, in a grown woman's belongings is quite unique." He restrained a smirk as he threw it on the bed.

"Your toiletries are packed away in the bathroom. Dinner is at seven in the kitchen. The master is at a charity dinner tonight, so it will just be Zander and yourself. You can call me at any time on the intercom if you need anything."

"Thank you, Steffen. I'll be down for dinner."

Waiting till I had the room to myself, I acquainted myself with where everything was, rearranging things to my liking. I still had an hour until dinner. Collecting my cello, I sat on the bed and started playing Dvořák Cello Concerto in B minor op.104. It had been months since I'd played this piece, but I felt it was right for tonight.

***

Spinning, I fell. The silk grabbed around my ankles and stopped me falling to Earth, allowing me to fly for a moment. I hung there for a little longer then grabbed a handful of the silk, untangled my ankles and started my slow controlled descent to Earth.

"That was great, Mora. You have great confidence up there. Just make sure you have the silk tight on your ankles before you drop," my instructor critiqued as I reached the bottom. "I'll see you on Wednesday?"

"Provided work doesn't keep me away." I waved goodnight, jogging to collect my bag from the corner.

"Not what I expected when Warren told me you were at the gym." Zander pushed off the wall next to my bag as I approached.

"It's a harder work out than any gym could give me," I replied toweling off, then pulled my pants and top on over my leotard and footless tights. "What are you doing here?"

"It's late. Dare doesn't want you on public transport this late. He sent me to pick you up."

"Dare?"

"Short for Darius."

"If you say so. Is he home already?" I put my watch back on. It was only ten, still early really.

"An hour now. He's not one for staying out partying all night. He makes sure his work goes off without a hitch and then comes home to the sanctity of his library." Zander waited till I buckled up my jacket and swung my bag over my shoulder before he opened the door and followed me out to the car park. "He got in and found out you weren't home and sent me out to find you. He was worried."

"I'm a big girl." I smiled, touched by their concern.

"That just makes you a target for a bigger predator," Zander replied flatly. "From now on, I'll be here to pick you up after training. Let me know the times tomorrow and I'll get you here and back."

"That's an hour and a half out of your night, two if you add travel time. That's not fair on you."

Zander held up a book as we reached his range rover. "I'm a reader. Doesn't matter much if it's here or in the sitting room."

I hopped in the front seat next to Zander. Starting the engine, he looked at me. "If you're going out at night, you let us know. Dare takes care of his staff, but you're the first female we've ever had live with us. Get ready to be big brothered to death."

Chapter Four

"So," Jasper started, his finger drawing lazily over my back. "Two weeks in. Are you happy with the new job?"

"So far, so good." I yawned laying my head on the pillow.

"No more verbal diarrhea in front of the illustrious Darius Rafal?" They were in the same industry, in a way, I'm sure they'd crossed paths before.

"No. I've barely seen him to tell the truth. I mainly deal with Warren and he's great."

Jasper licked up my spine. "And the new accommodations?" His breath blowing over the wet trail sent shivers up my spine.

Smiling, I recognized the signals that he was ready to go again. "Still luxurious and beautiful."

"You should sneak me in for a visit."

Rolling over, I pushed Jasper onto his back. "I signed a contract of non-disclosure. One of those terms was that I can't bring my lovers into his house."

I kissed his full lips, the taste of me still on his tongue. Squirming my way down his body, I took his growing cock in hand. Jasper lay back, placing his hands behind his head, so he could look down his body and watch while I sucked him.

Flicking the tip of him with my tongue, I smiled as his eyelids fluttered. Happiness surged through me as I swallowed him down, engulfing him. My stomach flipping and flopping as I sucked eagerly, enjoying the expressions on his face, the smooth feel of him in my mouth, the salty taste of his precum on my tongue. I was hungry, ravenous, desperate to feel him spurt himself into my mouth.

A phone started ringing. Glancing over to see my work phone dancing across the bedside table, I groaned and pulled away, diving across the bed for the phone.

Jasper looked shocked. "Hell no, I was just on edge."

I slid my thumb across the screen to answer. "You're the one who asked about work," I grumbled as I put the phone to my ear. "What's up?"

I hadn't looked at the caller ID, I just assumed it was Warren or Zander, so was a bit surprised by the Scottish accent. "Miss Ellis."

A loud slap echoed through the room and I jumped. "Jesus!"

"No, Darius."

"Not you." Turning my head, I glared at Jasper as he landed another hard smack on my rear. I clenched my teeth to hold my tongue but groaned despite myself. "Shit, Jasper," I breathed. Another smack. "Fuck, I'm on the phone with my boss!"

"I can fix that." Snatching the phone out of my hand, Jasper spoke to it without lifting it to his ear. "She is here with me. It is a Saturday. You've already cut into her weekend last night. She will call you back in the morning."

He threw the phone aside while I stared at him wide-eyed. "Are you trying to get me fired?"

When Jasper smacked me again, I moaned long and hard. "You are too good to fire over a weekend fuck frenzy." He flipped me over, spread my legs, and slapped my clit hard.

I dug my nails into the bed sheets, back arching as that sting reverberated through me and my clit throbbed with want.

"I'm seriously wanting that frenzied fucking now." Jasper dragged his fingers through my throbbing folds. "Look how wet you are after a little spanking." Lowering his face, he dragged his stubbled chin over me. "Look at those muscles clench with the need to feel me inside you."

Jasper grabbed a condom, rolled it on and slid into me. I gripped his arms where he held himself above me. He started thrusting hard and fast. "God, I love your sweet tight cunt," he roared.

My body was lifting off the bed; both with my back arching, but also that feeling of weightlessness that comes over your body as you near orgasm. I dug my nails in as I closed in on my climax. Jasper pulled back, changed angle, and pressed just his head inside of me, right up against my good spot.

He started muttering all the dirty things he'd already done to me tonight. His hand reached between us to strum my clit, playing me perfectly to have me singing his praises. He swelled against my g spot and my body responded.

Grasping my chin, Jasper forced my eyes to his. They were bright green, indicating he was right on edge himself and just needed that little push over. "Can I?" He requested gently. I nodded. "Not good enough, Mora. You know the rules. You need to say it."

"Yes," I gasped.

"Yes, what?"

"Bleed me," I whimpered, his hand tight at my chin.

Opening the drawer on his bedside table, Jasper removed his kit. Shifting himself back into the right position, he rocked his hips, climbing me to my end while he ripped open an alcohol swab and wiped across the base of my breast. I opened my eyes to watch as he unsheathed the sterile scalpel blade. He hesitated, closing his eyes. Just the thought was enough to nearly bring him.

Pulsing against my g spot, Jasper took a breath and made a clean precise cut. Not deep, that was our deal. It had to be superficial and in a spot no one could see it if I was in swimwear. I cried out at the pain and not in the good way. Grunting, Jasper threw the blade aside, losing himself.

My eyes were still wide from the pain, but the feel of my hot blood against my skin, combined with the feel of Jasper's ejaculation was too good for my body and psyche to ignore. Opening my mouth, I came voicelessly, Jasper rocking his hips till my body relaxed beneath him.

Dropping his mouth, Jasper lapped at my blood. Not over the cut. That would be introducing the chance of infection. He lapped at the rivulets across my skin and moaned. "I love how your blood looks against your pale skin, Mora," he complimented as he withdrew from me.

Gasping, I rolled to the side. Jasper grabbed a swab from his kit and used it to prevent any runoff from staining his sheets. With practiced hands, he cleaned me up, closed the wound with two steristrips, slathered the Manuka wound gel over the cut to prevent infection, and covered it.

Jasper completed his medical degree at Oxford University, but after completing his residency, ditched it to open his own night club. As far as he was concerned, he'd done as his parents requested; he was a qualified doctor. That he didn't work as one and became successful in the nightclub scene was his parents' issue, not his.

As far as blood play was concerned, Jasper and I were mild. I wouldn't have trusted anyone else with my health and well-being like this.

Once I was fixed, Jasper took the used swabs and scalpel and disposed of them properly before showering. Blood play wasn't a regular event for us, it'd been months since the last time. While the bleeding was a thing for me, it was more the trust I was placing in him, that did it for Jasper.

Just drifting off to sleep, I spied my phone on the floor. With great effort, I forced myself to my feet and retrieved it. There was a message from Darius.

Call me now!

With a groan, I dialed his number. "I'm really sorry," I apologised as soon as the ringing stopped.

"Warren said you bought home the mock ups for the Guy Fawkes Carnival yesterday."

"Yes. I was going over the plan like you asked. It's on my bedside table with my notes if you need it tonight."

"Thank you." Darius paused, the anger evident in his voice. "I don't need to say I'm not impressed with your boyfriend."

"It won't happen again." Next time I just wouldn't answer the phone.

"Good. And, Miss Ellis?"

"Yes, boss."

"When you get home tomorrow, we are going to sit down and have a talk about what I heard this evening."

"Heard?" I didn't need to look in the mirror to know the blood just drained from my face.

"I'll see you tomorrow for dinner."

It took me a moment to take the phone away from my ear. Boneless with shock, I collapsed on the bed.

"Everything good with the boss?" Jasper crawled onto the bed behind me, putting my phone back on the bedside table for me and turning my face to kiss me. He touched my face gently, worry etching his face. "What's wrong, baby?"

"You did hang up the phone before you threw it right?"

Jasper frowned deep in thought. After a moment, he hung his head. "Fuck!"

***

Opening the door to the apartment, I stopped. I was surprised by how quiet it was. Moving into the reception area, I expected to find Zander reading, but the place seemed deserted. Going towards the stairs to my room, I heard the soft music playing in the library. Taking a deep breath, I stepped into the room. Darius sat there reading a book. Steffen was pouring tea, two cups.

"Miss Ellis, join me please." Darius closed his book and set it aside. "Thank you, Steffen."

Giving a short nod, Steffen left the room, shutting the door on the way out. I slipped my bag from my shoulder, leaving it by the door, and moved to sit with him on the couch. Accepting the offered cup of tea, I took one sip and placed it aside. Sencha just wasn't my cup of tea.

"How did you end up in England, Mora?" Darius asked. He sat back, arms open and resting on the chair arms. His black polo shirt and gray chinos made him look the most relaxed I'd seen him since the day he offered me the job.

"I don't see how that's..."

"Humor me," Darius cut in and gave me a rare smile.

I took a deep breath. "My mother sent me here for my father to deal with."

"Your father is English?"

"Yes."

"How old were you?"

"Seventeen. I'd just finished high school, so the timing worked for going to college."

"Your father pulled some strings and got you into Cambridge?"

"No. I did that. My mother never went to Cambridge, she wasn't good enough to get in. I applied just to stick it to her. I came home from my last day of school to find my bags packed, a plane ticket and my already opened mid-year acceptance letter on my bed."

"Had you met your father prior to arriving in London?"

"No."

"So, you were effectively kicked out of your mother's house and sent to live with a strange man?"

"Basically."

Darius sat watching me. "Blood play is rare even in the BDSM world."

"The what?" I frowned.

Darius frowned. "You have heard of BDSM?" I shook my head. "It is an overlapping acronym. Bondage and Discipline, Domination and Submission, Sadism and Masochism."

"Oh, I just knew it as S and M." I bit my lip. "Look, you weren't meant to hear that last night. We were a bit caught up in things and Jasper forgot to hang up the phone."

Darius raised an eyebrow. "I am well aware I wasn't meant to hear that, Mora."

He called me by my first name. It sounded good. Why did it sound so good rolling from his tongue?

"Your fidgeting with the hem of your skirt would be a physical indicator of that." Darius sat forward. "As I was saying, blood play is very rare. In my experience, the women who enjoy it are also self-harmers." I looked away. "Strip."

That got my attention. "Excuse me?"

"I told you to take off your clothes."

"No." I stood to leave.

Darius hung his head a moment, then stood, pulling me to him and kissed me passionately. For a gut-wrenching moment, I fell into that kiss, and bizarrely, I felt I was finally somewhere I belonged. Then my brain kicked back into gear and I shoved him away from me.

"I am not my mother's daughter!" I yelled at him and ran from the library.

Running up to my room, I slammed the door behind me. I swiped at the tears that fell unbidden. Cursing, I took a deep breath. I was going to have to apologize to Darius a second time in twenty-four hours. If I still had a job in the morning, I'd be surprised.

Collecting my cello, I began playing an aggressive heavy metal song. The piece was heavy and violent and everything I needed to purge my anger. It worked my entire body better than a run would have. My fingers worked the fingerboard, my wrist worked quickly to change from up-bow to down-bow and back again in quick succession. Beads of perspiration covered my bare skin as I drew the bow across the strings for the final note, my left forearm working to create a vibrato.

Movement at the terrace doors caught my eye. Zander was standing on the terrace. Standing with surprise, I dropped the bow. Zander didn't hesitate. He opened the doors, walked straight up to me and wrapped me in a bear hug. Removing the neck of my cello from my hand, Zander placed it back in its stand and held me tight till my breathing evened out.

When I calmed, Zander stepped away. He took my hand and walked me to the far end of the terrace. Around the corner, the terrace opened to a much larger area and housed an outdoor table and chair set. Setting me down on the chair, he stepped inside the open doors at this end.

Peeking inside, I noted it was a bedroom. By the way he was rooting around in the wardrobe, I'd say it was his. Zander came back with a bottle of Finnish vodka. After taking the cap off, he handed it to me. Throwing back a mouthful, it burned down my throat. I didn't hand the bottle back, and he didn't ask for it. Zander just sunk onto the chair beside me, letting his arm run along the back of my chair.

After another swig of the vodka, I put the bottle on the table. "Thanks. This is the boys end is it?"

"You can come here anytime too."

"It's beautiful up here. So peaceful, like being set apart from the world."

Zander looked down at me as he ran a hand through my hair, brushing it back from my face. Shifting my chair against his, he took my shoulder in hand and pulled me closer to him. "It's also cold."

Snuggling into his side, we sat there quiet, watching the sunset. "I have never heard Bruce Dickinson played on cello before. Chemical Wedding, right?"

"You recognized it?" I smiled internally.

"It was a very good rendition. The way you played that riff, it's impressive on guitar, but watching your fingers move. I was sort of in awe."

"If it wasn't forbidden, I'd kiss you right now." I nudged him with my shoulder and Zander chuckled.

A buzzer sounded in Zander's room not long after the sun descended. I expected Zander to answer it, instead he hugged me tighter. "You're not what he expected. He thought he had your ticket. That's proving not to be the case."

I frowned. "So, kissing me was a test?"

Zander tensed. "That depends on where he kissed you."

"In the library." Zander raised a brow at me, a glint in his eye. "Oh. You meant—on the mouth, where else would he kiss me?"

Zander once again gave me that look, the side of his mouth pulling up at the side.

"Zander! That's just so inappropriate." I smacked his arm.

"Honey, that bruise on your shoulder, and the ones you came home with last week, tell me you get up to a whole lot of inappropriate on the weekend. Do not act innocent with me."

Blushing, I took a moment to compose myself, and stuck out my chin. "So?"

Zander sighed. "If he was testing you, he would never kiss your mouth. If he wanted sex from you, you would still be down there with his head between your thighs. If he kissed your mouth, he wanted something else from you."

"He wanted me to strip," I growled.

"Why?" Zander didn't act shocked by the request.

"What do you mean why?"

"He asked you to strip, you refused. The kiss was to seduce you to the point he would get what he wanted, which was to see you naked. He would have kept his clothes on, seen what he wanted to see and walked away." Zander looked down, meeting my eyes. "So why did he want to see you naked. Does he think you are on drugs?"

"No." I looked at him disgusted. With a sigh I ran over the conversation looking for the information. I closed my eyes when I caught on. "He thinks I'm into self-mutilation."

Zander looked back out at the lights of the city in the distance. "Are you?"

"No."

The buzzer sounded again. Zander sighed, standing up. "Go tell him what he wants to know."

"I guess apologizing sooner is better than later."

Zander shook his head. "Do not apologize. He should not have kissed you like that. He owes you the apology."

"Do you think I'll get it?"

Zander laughed. "Uh, no." He walked into his room, shutting the doors before going to the intercom and picking up the handset.

Making my way to my bedroom, I stepped back inside and closed the doors. Opening my bedroom door to walk out, I found Darius standing on the landing, his hand raised to knock. He lifted my bag. "You left this down stairs."

"Thank you." Taking the bag, I stepped back into my room, dropping it on my bed. Darius stayed in the entry way. "Come in."

Darius came in and shut the door behind him before crossing his arms.

"I used to cut myself when I was younger, but you can barely see any sign of that now. I wasn't hacking at my flesh or anything. I just liked to see my blood running free, to feel all those painful emotions I couldn't express running out of me. It wasn't to commit suicide or disfigure myself. I never put my life at risk."

Darius searched my eyes as if unsure he believed what I was saying.

"You could have just asked me. Asking me to strip was uncalled for. Kissing me to achieve that same outcome was unprofessional and below the belt. You would have left me feeling exposed and that would not be conducive to a good working environment."

Darius tilted his head, his eyes narrowing in on me as I spoke.

I sighed. "From now on, you want to know something, ask me straight out. I'll be honest. If I don't want to tell you, I'll tell you it's none of your business. Deal?"

Darius stepped closer. "You got upset at me downstairs because of your mother. Why?"

I sat on my bed. "My mother had an affair with the director of the company she interned for during her last year in college. I'm the result."

Darius shifted his stance, shoving his hands in his pockets. "Do you ensure safe practice during blood play?"

He was worried for my well-being. It was kind of sweet. "Jasper is a qualified medical practitioner. Everything is sterile, only I bleed, so there is no cross contamination. The cut is always superficial. It heals quickly and has minimal scarring."

"He also hits you," Darius began.

"He spanks me," I corrected. "We have a contract, a safe word, hard and soft limits are clearly defined. He talks me through anything new which may push a soft limit."

Darius exhaled like he was relieved. After a moment, he met my eyes. "Add that he is not to touch your phone to the contract please, as a hard limit." Darius turned to leave.

"He was right." Darius looked over his shoulder at me. "It was my time. I was away from work. You could have sent a message and I would have replied as soon as I could."

Darius turned back to me. "You were aware out of hours work would be required when you took the job."

"And you were aware I spend my weekends relieving the stress of the work week. You knew where I was last night. I don't think you had to guess what I would be doing."

His nostrils flared, eyes dark and hard. "Might I suggest, in the future, if you are in the midst of your stress release, you do not answer the phone. Dinner is ready." He walked out.

I swear he wasn't angry about hearing me have sex, but that I didn't want him to ring me. Darius wasn't the only person suffering head spins trying to work someone out.

Chapter Five

"Grab your stuff," Warren instructed as he walked back to his desk from the elevator. "Dare has a walk-through at the new function center."

Locking my computer, I grabbed my bag. "Which center?"

Warren grabbed his folio case and phone. "His. Renovations are wrapping up and he wants to ensure they are up to scratch. We are meeting him downstairs."

Lynwood Corporation was expanding. After years of hiring other facilities, Lynwood Corporation purchased an old mill, renovated it, and would be hiring it out for weddings and conferences. I'd seen the plans when I came to work here two months ago, so I couldn't wait to see the finished product.

"I'll meet you down there." I started toward the fire exit.

The fact I would opt for the stairs had been accepted and not pushed. If he could, Warren would give me advance notice, so I could factor in the extra time for taking the stairs. At times like this, it was just best to get down them as quickly as possible so that Darius wasn't kept waiting.

Exiting into the foyer, I spied Darius talking to one of his managers. Darius's eyes tracked me through the foyer as I moved to the exit and the waiting car. I knew the routine well now. Never interrupt unless it was something he needed. If Darius wanted me for anything, he'd let me know.

Clark saw me coming and opened the back door. "There will be three of us, Clark. I might sit up front with you if you don't mind."

Clark smiled shutting the door and opened the front passenger door.

"Thanks, Clark," Warren spoke over my shoulder, stepping past me and into the front passenger seat.

"Hey, I called shotgun."

Warren grinned at me. "What the hell is shotgun?"

He was taking the mickey. I knew it. He'd been making fun of my Australian colloquialisms for two months now. With clenched fists, I stepped back to the back door as Darius approached.

Clark paused for a moment then shut the front door and opened the back door again. Climbing in, I slid across so Darius could get in. I was adjusting my skirt when Darius dropped onto the seat. Noticing my hands, he turned his attention to his seatbelt causing me to start laughing.

Warren turned around. "What's so funny?"

"Just a memory."

Warren quirked a brow in humor. "Good memory?"

"Not the memory itself so much, as my naivety. I thought being in that back seat letting a guy kiss and feel me beneath my skirt was so rebellious only five years ago." I sighed. "My innocence was ridiculous."

Darius's fingers gripped a piece of paper, his jaw tensing as he handed me a list. "Look that over and let me know if you see any issues."

Taking the list, I started scanning through the names of performers for the New Year's Eve celebrations. A name halfway down the list caught my attention. I scanned back up the list. "This will be a problem. You can't have Cindy Curtis and Michael Boon at the same event anytime soon. Dump Cindy and pull in that new local singer, Evelina."

Darius took the list back from me. "Why would Cindy and Michael be problematic? They're engaged aren't they?"

"Were engaged. She was at the club on Friday, drunk and dry humping one of the Sector brothers. She went home with him too. People were taking photos on their phones and posting it. I give it a week till the break up is announced, but that's beside the point. She's having substance abuse issues and spiraling into a dark place.

"Her agent needs to pull her off the scene and get her some help or she's going to end up being another Winehouse. Dump her and keep her off the list till she gets her act cleaned up," I offered as my personal phone started buzzing.

Darius scratched Cindy from the list and handed it to Warren. "That's good to go then."

Warren nodded, taking the list and opening his tablet to adjust the digital list.

Silencing the alarm on my personal phone, I sighed. "I have to make a call." Pressing dial, I put the phone to my ear.

"Liza Ellis's phone," a chirpy voice sang at the other end of the line.

"Hi, Gerry. Is the Wicked Witch available?" I asked my mother's personal assistant.

"Mora. Oh my God, it's great to hear your voice," she chimed. "She's with guests and doesn't want to be disturbed."

"Of course, she doesn't. God forbid she take a call from her own daughter. Wish her a happy birthday for me."

"I will. How's London?" Gerry asked conversationally.

"London is good," the buildings blurring past the window as we drove.

Gerry had been my mother's personal assistant since I was twelve. She stopped trying to get my mother to take my calls by the time I was fourteen. We were both resigned to the fact that the quick chats with Gerry were the closest I was going to get to having a relationship with my mother.

"So, what did I get the Witch? Please tell me it was the new broomstick I asked you to get her?"

Gerry laughed. "Close. Skydiving lessons."

Pausing, I checked my phone. "I'm sorry. Did you say I, Mora, the most hated daughter on Earth, got her skydiving lessons? As in, someone is going to push my mother out of a plane, several thousand feet above the Earth, and yell happy birthday from Mora, as she plummets to her potential death?"

Gerry was laughing loudly now. "Exactly. It's what she wanted."

I took an excited breath. "That is awesome, Gerry. Can I add one more thing? Can you hand her a broomstick as she boards the plane and tell her it's in case her parachute fails?"

"I've got to go, Mora. I'll film it for you."

"Sure, just stop filming before the chute opens. I'll let my imagination fill in what happens after."

Gerry guffawed and hung up the phone. I smiled wistfully as I gazed out the window for a moment, then shoved my phone away. Darius and Warren were looking at me.

"Sorry. It's my mother's birthday."

Darius looked back at his iPad. "She was too busy to talk to you tonight?"

I laughed. "She hasn't taken a phone call from me, well, ever."

"Does she call you for your birthday?" Warren queried with a frown.

"No, but I make it a point to call her every year. I know it annoys the hell out of her to be reminded of me when she's enjoying herself." I swallowed the anger in my throat. "I'm actually going to record myself singing happy birthday, and pay someone to call her every year after I die, so that she thinks I'm haunting her from my grave."

"You think she will outlive you?" Warren looked concerned.

I laughed. "I know it. Only the good die young. That woman is evil incarnate."

"A lot of women who are very successful business women are perceived in that manner," Darius defended. "People make great sacrifices to get to the top."

"Successful business people sacrifice love," I responded quietly. Warren's eyes flicked warily to Darius and back. "The love of a good relationship doesn't exist for them because they are unable to trust. The love of their children suffers, because they are too busy clawing over their colleagues to bother with their kids. Successful business people fail at successful, healthy, relationships."

"Her career success paid for your Cambridge education." Darius slid his iPad away, the tenseness of his jaw indicating that he'd taken my remark personally.

"I was on full scholarship and worked behind a bar to pay my way. My father paid for my schooling and extracurricular activities growing up, and his child support probably covered the food I ate and clothes I wore. That woman didn't contribute anything but the stretch marks of pregnancy toward me."

"Have you ever made those comments about the broomstick to her face?" Darius asked carefully.

I smiled, pure joy flooding my system at the memory. "I gave her a broomstick with her name engraved in it when she forgot my sixteenth birthday. Whenever I need a happy moment, I think of her face when she unwrapped it." I returned to looking out the window, rain starting to spatter the window. "It's my favorite childhood memory."

Clark exhaled. "I bet this rain makes you miss home, Miss Ellis?"

"Home is where the heart is, Clark, which is definitely not where I grew up."

We pulled into the car park of an old industrial building. Darius and Warren opened their doors to exit. Clark opened mine and gave me his hand to help me out, holding an umbrella over my head. "Take it." Clark smiled sadly handing it to me.

"Mr. Rafal." A man in his early thirties, suffering from early pattern baldness, rushed out of the large glass doors, a large umbrella held aloft. Darius stepped underneath and walked with him inside.

Walking around the front of the car, I came to stand with Warren. He smiled at me and we followed our boss. When we stepped inside, I paused. The inside was full of luxurious lounges set by a large unlit double-sided fire place, a large bar to one side. The decor was all gold and cream, it looked beautiful.

"As you can see, the reception area is complete as per the specifications," the man spoke anxiously as he dropped his folded umbrella into a holder by the door.

Folding my umbrella, I stuck it in the same holder. Darius walked forward into the reception area and started inspecting everything. He sat on the lounges, smacked a few cushions around, tugged on the gold silk curtains, knocked on the double hung windows. When he seemed satisfied, he started toward an arched doorway.

"I want to see the fireplaces working before I leave," Darius directed as he passed.

The balding man bobbed his head and ran off through a staff-only door. Warren and I followed Darius into a large foyer. It had dark timber paneling on the wall, which matched the timber flooring. There were three sets of double doors along the long corridor. Darius walked to the first and opened the doors, stepping inside. I followed, Warren behind me.

This room was set up in a classroom manner for corporate conferences, easily seating fifty people. The gold and cream decor flowed in waves through the room. Darius moved into the room and sat at one of the back tables.

"Mora, could you go to the podium and test out the system please?" Darius requested.

Moving to the front of the room, hit the button to power up the controls on the podium, and started playing. I turned on the microphone. "These controls are fairly user friendly," I stated clearly. I dimmed the lights, lowered the overhead projector screen and switched on the projector. Everything about the space screamed luxury and success.

Darius was saying something to Warren who typed notes quickly into his iPad. After a moment Darius stood. I took the cue and turned everything off at the podium. Darius was already out the door and opening the next door when I walked out of the room, Warren holding the door for me. The next room was similar, but set up with round tables. It allowed room for an adequate dance space. I would call it a multi-functional function room. Again, I was asked to test the digital equipment while Warren took notes.

The third space was the largest. It was very obviously the place for large fairy-tale weddings or big charity balls. Glass doors all along the side looked out over a courtyard garden that was stunningly landscaped. The place screamed opulence and I had no doubt it already had a twelve-month waiting list for availability. Baldy came back and the large fireplace along one wall ignited.

At the dance floor end hung long gold silks as a decoration on either end of the stage. Approaching, I gave them a tug.

"What are you doing?" Baldy looked ready to have a heart attack.

"What any child between two and sixteen is going to do," I responded without looking at him. "Was a risk assessment done on these?"

Baldy threw his chin up, hands on his hips and his voice went up an octave. "Yes, of course, not that this is the sort of place you'd bring children."

I raised a brow. "This is exactly the sort of place you are going to get children who are left to run unsupervised while their parents have a good time. What is the weight bearing?" Giving the silk another tug, Darius and Warren joined us and were listening with interest.

"Two hundred kilos," baldy answered flabbergasted. He turned to address Darius.

Dropping my bag to the ground, I kicked off my shoes and removed my jacket. Baldy saw me and went pale. "What do you think..."

Wrapping my wrists in one of each of the silks above head height, I pulled myself off the ground testing the hold. It held me. Unable to resist, I pulled my body up past my hands and into a handstand. Yes, I was wearing a skirt. Yes, gravity took effect. I didn't care, I was flying.

Wrapping my legs in the silk, I released my wrists and, using my abs, pulled myself up to grab the silk above my feet. Releasing my legs, I held the silk across the belt of my back and swung.

"Stop that!" Baldy yelled at me.

Happy that it held my weight and I was able to swing on it safely, I slid back to the ground, righted my clothing and slipped back into my shoes.

"What do you think you were doing?" Baldy got in my face.

"Ensuring Mr. Rafal doesn't end up with a lawsuit on his hands because someone gets drunk and decides to play Tarzan across the dance floor," I answered evenly. Stepping into baldy, I looked him up and down. "Of course, that's all going to depend on how big Tarzan is, isn't it?"

Spinning on my heel, I opened the door to the garden, walking out and following the path to reach the other side. I was not bothered by the slightly heavier rain. There were glass doors on the other side and I figured there was another room still to be checked.

Entering the other building with its modest oriental décor, I instantly recognized it for what it was. Slipping again out of my shoes, I left them and my bag by the door and moved into the meditation space. These were becoming all the rage with big companies. Studies showed that people in high stress jobs who meditated, were better able to handle their jobs, and less likely to keel over from a heart attack.

It made sense that Darius would have one built into his conference center. You could bring your staff in for a work conference and include a session on learning to meditate at the same time. Approaching the table at the front of the room, I removed an incense stick and lit it before placing it in the holder. Taking a few steps back to the first cushion, I sat myself down, taking up a full lotus pose and starting the deep breathing practice of meditation.

"Is it comfortable?" Darius asked standing next to me.

"Try it and tell me what you think?" I answered keeping my eyes closed.

The heat of Darius body lowering to the cushion beside me pushed against me, forcing me to take several deep breaths. "That incense stinks," he huffed.

"It's wrong for meditation," I responded slowly opening my eyes. "While the cushions for the most part are fine, they aren't going to cut if for the more over indulgent employees coming through here."

"You think something a little cushier?" Darius was already standing again. He offered his hand and I let him help me up.

"And add a water feature out in the garden. The sound of running water is quite relaxing," I suggested, taking my hand back. As I did, the gentle rain became a torrential downpour.

Darius looked out the doors. "And a cover so that people can walk between the buildings without getting wet," he sighed.

Walking back to the door, I watched the rain come down. "We could stay out here till it slows. Practice some meditation ourselves."

Darius graced me with a smile. "As nice as that sounds, I have another meeting in an hour."

Slipping on my shoes, I collected my bag. "Guess we're getting wet then."

Darius's pupils dilated. I winked before moving out into the rain to walk around to the main building. I didn't run, it was well known that running in rain only resulted in you being drenched, not that there was anything not drenched on me as I walked into the timber foyer from the courtyard door.

Warren was there when I stepped inside, his eyes instantly tracking to my blouse. "We might need to get you a new blouse before we go to the next meeting."

Clearing my throat, I buttoned my jacket up covering the sheer, now transparent, pale gray cotton. "I think I need an entire new outfit. I'm drenched."

"Which is why I was on my way over with this." Warren held up the umbrella. "I'll go get the boss."

He stepped past me with a sneaky smile. I cursed under my breath, of course Darius waited. He knew Warren would bring the umbrella. Oh well. Too late now. Squelching my way to the front door, I collected Clark's umbrella and continued out to the car.

When I knocked on his window, Clark let it down an inch. "Do you have a towel? I got drenched and don't want to sit on the seat wet."

"I have my gym bag in the boot. There is a towel in that."

He moved to get out. I held up my hand. "Don't. I'm already wet."

At the boot, I lifted the tail gate and found the towel. Closing the boot, I opened the car door, spreading it on the back seat before hopping in. Taking out my compact, I wiped under my eyes with a tissue to remove the small amount of mascara that had run. I used a brush to quickly redo my hair in a high ponytail, and by the time I'd finished that, Darius was sliding into the backseat with me, still dry as a bone.

He looked me over and spoke to Clark. "Take us to Burberry, it is closest."

"Yes, Mr. Rafal."

I looked at him aghast. "I can't afford that place."

Darius pulled out his phone. "I know you can't." He took a breath. "Hi, Melisse, it's Darius Rafal. I need you to pick out a black, work appropriate dress, size ten, matching shoes, size nine, and a black trench coat. Charge it to my account. Mora will be there in ten minutes to pick it up. She will need to change into it in the store so remove the tags please," Darius smiled. "Yes, thank you, Melisse."

He hung up the phone and started discussing what still needed to be done at the new function center.

Twenty minutes later, I slid back into the back seat of the Rolls Royce in a black silk tunic dress, black leather ankle boots, and a black trench coat that easily cost half of my pay check by itself. Darius looked me over and smiled. "Thank you for being quick."

"I'm wearing two weeks' worth of pay here. I'm terrified I'll get it dirty."

Darius relaxed as Clark pulled us back into traffic. "Well, it suits you. I'm surprised, though. With who your mother is, I would have thought you grew up wearing this stuff."

"You missed the part about me being a rebellious brat of a child didn't you?"

Darius smirked. I returned it.

Chapter Six

"Miss Ellis," Steffen greeted me in the foyer when I got home that night. "You have a guest waiting in the reception room."

I frowned. Home on time for once this week, I was keen for a long hot bath after my time in the rain today. "Thanks, Steffen. Who is it?"

"A Mr. Hark. He has a package for you." Steffen turned toward the kitchen. "Will your guest be staying for dinner?"

"As much as I'd like that, I don't think the master would be happy with that." I missed spending time with Alex. When we worked together, we'd see each other daily, get dinner several times a week. Now, it was basically Friday nights at JJ's, and even that seemed limited.

Steffen raised a brow. "The restriction is on you having lovers over, Miss Ellis. He did not say you could not have friends visit. Is Mr. Hark a lover?"

My eyes widened. "Ah, no. Definitely not."

Steffen gave me a smile which suggested he was already aware that was the case. "Then I will set an extra place for dinner. We will eat at the dining table tonight I think." Steffen gave a polite bow of his head and toddled off to the kitchen.

With a smile, I stepped through the arch into the reception room. Alex was sitting on the black leather lounge by the fire. He lifted his head from his phone and smiled when he saw me. "Surprise!" He stood up.

I went to him and he pulled me into a big hug. "What brought this on?" I asked, happy for the affection.

Alex pulled back. "Well, firstly, that package arrived at work for you today and I thought I'd drop it off. Secondly, what kind of brother would I be not to inspect my baby sister's new abode?" Alex looked around the reception room and whistled. "Nice digs. Makes your old place look like a shack."

"It was cozy and I was happy there." I sat on the lounge.

Alex sat beside me, studying my face. "Are you happy here?"

"Most of the time," I replied honestly before turning my attention to the package. Sitting forward, I looked at the packing slip and frowned.

"Not what you were expecting?" Alex sat forward to join me.

"I wasn't expecting anything, especially from home." I pulled at the tape but it was well sealed.

"Here." Alex took his Swiss army knife out of his pocket and handed it to me.

Smiling, I flicked it open to cut the tape. Inside were some neatly packed items. Pulling out a soft koala toy, well-cuddled and loved, I set it aside. Next was a photo album. I didn't open it; I knew it was all my childhood photos. There were a few well wrapped crystal ornaments, and some vintage jewelery, all of which belonged to my grandmother. They were items of hers I'd spent hours admiring as a child. My dread was growing with each item.

As I reached the bottom of the box there was an envelope with my name on it and a beautifully presented booklet. Setting the envelope aside, I stared at the beautiful cursive script on the booklet.

In loving memory of Freida Mora Ellis.

The tears started falling as I read the funeral date of three months ago. Anger flooded me. "That bitch!" I hissed standing up, and retrieved my phone from my bag. Alex watched with worry, collecting the booklet and looking through it. I pressed in my mother's number and hit call.

"Liza Ellis's phone," Gerry answered immediately.

"Put her on," I growled.

"Mora?" Gerry queried, her voice worried. "She's at the gym. What's wrong?"

"Why didn't you tell me?"

"Tell you what, honey?" Gerry's voice was gentle. She knew, but was playing dumb. I knew her too well.

"About Nan?" I sobbed. "Why wasn't I told?"

Gerry took a deep breath. "Your mother told me not to call you. Said she would tell you herself."

"You knew that was bullshit, Gerry! You should have called me and told me so I could come home for the funeral."

"Mora, I'm really sorry. You know how it is. She's my boss."

"And that was my nan, the woman who raised me. You didn't even mention the package on the phone this morning."

"Mora, really, I'm so very sorry. Your mother was upset and..."

"Save it," I spat. "You've spent over a decade apologizing to me on her behalf. Just do me the courtesy of not bothering to tell me when that bitch dies either."

Disconnecting the call, I threw the phone at the lounge. Alex stood, pulling me into his arms and held me tight.

"Do you know, for the first six years of my life, I thought Nan was my mother. I thought Liza was an aunt who lived with me. I didn't realize that wasn't the case till I went to school and grandparents and parents were explained.

"I went home from my first day at school and asked my nan if I was an orphan and what happened to my parents. I spent the rest of my childhood pretending I was an orphan and that my two very loving parents had been taken from me by an act of God. It was easier than acknowledging I just wasn't wanted."

Alex massaged the back of my head with his strong fingers. "Your mother didn't want you. That's not the case for dad. When he found out about you, and that you were being raised by your grandmother, he tried to get custody. He took your mum to court. You were born in Australia and had never even met him. He lost. He was only allowed to see you from a distance, never allowed to talk to you. It was part of the agreement."

Lifting my head from his shoulder, I met Alex's eyes confused at hearing this for the first time. "Why didn't he tell me that when I first came here?"

Alex shrugged. "It was water under the bridge. He hoped you could get to know each other as adults, but you threw that wall of yours up and never gave him a chance. He probably would have written you off as a lost cause, except, you welcomed me into your life with an open heart. He saw how much it meant to you to have a brother and to be a part of my life." Alex smiled kindly and wiped the tears from my cheek. "We both knew then; you were just protecting yourself from another absent parent."

Alex took my hand and walked me back to the couch to sit. "Marshall has an entire photo album of you. He went to every dance recital, every sporting event, your high school graduation," Alex frowned. "He'd just stepped off the plane at Heathrow from your graduation when your mother called. She told him you'd been accepted to Cambridge and you were on the next plane to London. I believe her exact words were that he wanted you, he could have you.

"He took me to see you a couple of times," Alex smiled. "The court papers said Marshall couldn't talk to you, they didn't include me."

I frowned at Alex, not remembering him at all.

Alex chuckled. "You were ten the first time. Dad took me to Australia for a holiday. After a day of sightseeing, he took me to the library. I thought that was kind of boring after the day we'd had, I was seventeen after all. He pointed to this little girl with long black pigtails, quietly reading by herself in the corner." Alex gave my ponytail a gentle tug, causing me to smile.

"He told me you were my sister and then explained that he wasn't allowed to talk to you, but I could. I sat down beside you and asked about your book. You told me to get my own. I was smitten immediately. You had this real feisty attitude."

I smiled, that sounded just like me.

"Your nan was there. Marshall said she'd got in contact with him when you were six for some emergency. After that, she told him whenever you had a big event on. He called her when he was coming to town and they would arrange a place where he could come and see you."

"That sounds just like Nan." I thought about it. "There was an incident when I was six. I got badly hurt. She must have called to tell him."

Alex nodded. "He didn't even know you existed until that happened."

I blew out a breath. "I never really gave him a chance. I've been such a bitch to him."

Alex laughed. "That's nonsense. About the bitch part anyway." Alex turned to face me a little more. "Look, he gets it. He should have broken the rules and spoken to you. Your nan wanted him too, but he didn't know how to approach you after a while. What if you wanted to leave with him? He couldn't take you out of the country without your mother's approval, so he left it how it was. No one can blame you for being angry at him, but you've never been rude or reckless. You were a good kid, and a fairly responsible adult. He's very proud of the woman you've become, even if he can't take any of the credit for it."

Alex's eyes flicked over my head and I turned to see Steffen standing in the door way. He waited till we both knew he was there then came in with two wine glasses and a bottle of red.

"Why don't you and your guest go up to the rooftop and have a drink and relax? The others will be back from the gym shortly, and the brothers will want to socialize."

Smiling, I took the glasses and bottle from him. "Thanks, Steffen." He was moving us out of Darius's way.

Steffen nodded and left the room again.

I handed the glasses and bottle to Alex. "Come on. I'll show you the real beauty of this place."

Packing my inherited items back in the box, I led the way up to my room. Alex raised a brow and whistled again at my room. Leaving the box on the bed, I opened the balcony door, closing it after us and leading the way around to the terrace. Despite it being mid-summer, it was still chilly enough that I was glad I hadn't taken off my coat yet.

"Well this makes my place look like a hovel." Alex sighed, watching the city lights over the roof tops.

"I love your apartment. It's the perfect bachelor's pad for a man your age." I chuckled.

"I would like to point out your boss is a year younger than me and this is his bachelor's pad."

"Well, technically it's the bachelor pad for all three of them. I'm the only one not allowed to bring a lover back here."

Alex lifted a brow. "And why do you think that is?"

I shrugged. "Mr. Rafal is slightly sexist. Women must wear skirts or dresses, no pants at work. I would hasten a guess that his idea is that women of quality should not be screwing around, but waiting for their prince charming to come and save them from their tower and their virginity."

Alex laughed. "He was at JJ's with you the night before he hired you. If he saw you and Jasper together, I'm pretty sure he knows you are not a virgin."

"That he does." Darius's voice came from the side.

Alex and I turned to see Darius walking toward us from the direction of my room. He was freshly showered, hair still wet, his skin still a little damp. He wore jeans and a t-shirt, a real one, straining around his biceps and chest. He wasn't as built as Zander, but this outfit did nothing to hide his physique. In fact, it damn well highlighted his body with neon arrows that yelled *sex on legs*.

He pulled on a sweater as he walked toward us, his shirt lifting to glimpse his well-defined abdomen. I imagined biting my way across those abs. Abandoning that thought before it gathered steam, I focused on where he approached from.

"Did you come up here via my room?"

Darius took a seat opposite us. "Steffen informed me you had a guest. I came up to say hello."

"Via my bedroom?" I frowned at him. "Were you hoping to catch us having sex?"

"Definitely not." Darius shook his head at me. "You know my rules, since you were just explaining them to your friend." Darius looked at Alex. "Mr. Hark, a pleasure to see you again."

Alex nodded. "Mr. Rafal. I actually believe Mora was explaining the hypocrisy of your rules."

Darius frowned. "It's not up for debate. You want to have sex with her, it doesn't happen under my roof."

Alex cringed; I laughed. "You never have to worry about that with Alex and me. Our relationship is entirely sex free and always will be."

Darius quirked a brow. "And why is that?"

"I'm sorry?" Alex frowned.

"Why would you never have sex with Mora? She's beautiful, young, intelligent..."

"Related to me," Alex finished pointedly. "Incest is not something practiced here in Western society."

Darius looked between us. "You're related?"

"On my father's side," I clarified for him, without answering the real question he was asking, which was how. "So, you can chill about Alex and I spending alone time together."

"Actually, you only have to keep Jasper out," Alex added.

Darius raised that brow in question again. Slapping Alex's arm, I hushed him, to no avail.

"She's only been with Jasper. He was her first and only. One day he'll get sick of playing the field and they'll marry and have babies."

"Jasper was not my first," I argued.

Alex sat straighter with interest. "Really? Because I was sure you were a virgin when you arrived in England."

I blushed. "Yes, well, I was."

"And I knew the night Jasper got in your knickers for the first time, because I was there at the club when he took you home."

"I remember," I groaned.

"So, you were pretty busy with college and working." Alex paused for effect. "When did you find time to meet the one, lose your virginity, and break up with him?"

With both men watching me intently, I blushed really hard. Darius especially. I cleared my throat. "Look, there was a guy I met at one of the charity events dad took me to a couple of months after I got here.”

“You lost your virginity on a one-night stand?” Darius asked, voice low and unhappy.

I fidgeted. “Don’t call it that. It wasn’t like that.”

Darius crossed his arms. “What was it like?”

Swallowing, I glanced away from those bunching muscles. “I didn’t intend to sleep with him. I saw him, knew my flirting with him would goad my father and went for it. We danced a couple of times. We talked. We went our separate ways.”

“How did dancing and talking lead to sex?” Alex queried, enjoying getting the story from me finally.

I sighed. “Dad saw me dancing with him and got angry, as I expected. He told me to leave. I think dad thought if I left then, I couldn’t get into any more trouble. I ran into the guy at the front door. He kissed me good night.” I closed my eyes at the memory. “It felt right.”

Opening my eyes, I met Darius’s. He was studying me, as if he couldn’t figure me out. “Do you regret it? That being your first time?” Darius asked.

“No,” I answered factually. “Despite the circumstances, what came before, what came after, it was perfect, so much more than I’d imagined it.”

Darius blinked. I’d surprised him.

“Please tell me it was not some old cretin or power-hungry asshole.” Alex sounded appalled.

I laughed. “Not an old cretin. When I met him, he was just a nice guy who kissed really well.”

“What happened,” Darius was still assessing me, “after?”

I fidgeted with the hem of my skirt. “He fell asleep. I got dressed and went home.”

“What was his name?” Alex glared.

I shook my head. “It doesn’t matter.”

“It does matter, Mora. For guys it’s different. We are so keen to start having sex we would screw the lunch lady to lose the big V,” Alex argued exasperated.

"Speak for yourself," Darius cut in. "My lunch lady was hideous."

I smirked. Alex tipped my chin toward him. "It's different for girls. You are never getting that back. It should have been someone special, someone who meant something to you. You were seventeen. He took advantage of you and I will kill him for it," Alex growled angrily.

"He was special, Alex," I beseeched. "He was the first person who made me feel like I belonged, like I was special, and that I was wanted. The words he said to me that night meant something to me. I wanted to be with him, if only to hold that gift of belonging inside me a little longer." I unclenched my fist from my chest. How could I explain to my brother that I loved that man, for only one night, but it was the love of a lifetime I felt for those few special hours.

"Who was it?" Alex pushed, but there was gentleness in the request now.

I exhaled. "I'm not going to tell you, Alex. That night is sacred to me." I closed my eyes brushing my thumb over my lips. "The way he kissed me." My hands caressed down my neck. "The way he touched me. The way he looked at me." I opened my eyes. "The words he murmured to me."

Darius shifted in his seat, his head cocked to the side still studying me.

Alex sat back. "Do you need to go to your room and have some alone time?"

Smirking, I picked up my wine glass and took a drink. "No. I'll take care of myself later. I actually didn't start masturbating till after that night, and I tell you now, even as a memory, that man brought me to my first orgasm."

Alex stuck his fingers in his ears. "Oh, my God. No wonder you had to move out of dad's."

Darius sat up straight. "You are brother and sister."

Alex closed his eyes realizing his mess up. When they opened it was to look at me. Meeting his eyes, I asked my question. Alex shook his head slightly. We both sighed with relief. No one knew who my father was, not many more knew who Alex's was.

"Yes." Alex sighed lifting his glass of wine to his lips. "Mora is my baby sister from a different mother."

The door to Zander's room opened and he switched on his bedroom light. He was still in his gym gear looking sufficiently worked out. I watched as he pulled the shirt over his head throwing it in his laundry basket as he walked to the bathroom and shut the door. I sighed with a sensual smile.

"Perv." Alex jabbed me in the ribs with his elbow.

"Yep!" I took another drink of the wine.

Darius looked up and realized we were sitting in the dark. "I might need to install a sensor light out here so Zander is aware when he has an audience."

I chuckled. "He knows. That's why he kept his pants on and went into the bathroom to strip. It's also why he shut the door."

Darius glared across the table. "I take it that was a lesson learned?" I shrugged. Darius clenched his teeth. "He looks at you like a younger sister."

"Which I'm happy for him to do. I'm not wanting anything to happen between us. I just like to admire a very well-developed physique. Most of the guys at work think putting on a suit is all the sex appeal they need." I sat forward topping up my empty glass.

Alex frowned. "The suit works, Mora. Trust me."

I looked at him. "I've noticed. Tell me, how are things with your girlfriend and mistress?"

Alex growled. "Leila wants to move in with me. Sophie wants… more."

Darius sat forward. "In my observations of other people's relationships, cheating never ends well."

"I always thought that. Sophie just happened," Alex said into his wine. "And then she happened more regularly."

"Be careful, Alex. That's my best friend you are talking about," I grumbled.

"Which is how, I am guessing, she became a mistress instead of just a one night escape," Darius sympathized.

Alex stayed quiet, not answering.

I shook my head. "Just end it with one or both of them, Alex. The longer you leave it, the worse it's going to get. Sophie's my friend. I'll be forced to hate you if you hurt her badly."

Zander's glass doors opened. "Hey, I didn't know there was a party up here tonight," Zander smiled taking in the extras.

Most nights, it would just be Zander, Warren and I up here talking, or in the media room watching a movie together. In the two months I'd been living here, I'd spent a lot of time with the brothers and grown close to Zander in particular. He really did treat me like a loving big brother. He reminded me of Alex a lot that way.

Zander took in Darius's presence but didn't make a big deal out of it. Instead, he walked to Alex. "Hi, I'm Zander Mann. Who are you and what are you doing with my little sister?"

Alex raised a brow and laughed. "Strange, I don't remember having any brothers." Darius knew now, there was no point hiding it from the brothers.

Zander's smile fell. It made me smile. "Zander, this *is* my brother, Alex Hark."

We spent another thirty minutes chatting. Zander and Alex were a lot alike and got along well. We joked and discussed our days. Darius sat there, occasionally contributing to the conversation, but mainly just observing. His eyes were heat across my skin whenever he sat watching me. Eventually, Warren came out, also freshly showered and informed us dinner was ready.

After dinner Alex left. Retreating to my room, I sat on my bed staring at the few items of my grandmother's possessions I'd received. I hadn't kept in contact, so it was just as much my fault that it took me three months to find out she passed away. I'd call her for her birthday, and a few other times throughout the year, but I'd let the ball drop.

A knock at my door pulled me back to the present. "Come in," I called, gently packing the items back in the box.

Darius stepped in, leaving the door ajar. He watched me pack away the items. He stepped forward collecting the koala off the bed. "Steffen told me you were crying earlier, that an angry phone call ensued and your guest needed to calm you down. It's why I came up to check on you earlier, Mora, not to enforce my rules. You are an honorable woman, you would not risk your job and reputation for sex."

I wiped the last of the tears from my cheek. "Thank you. I'll apologize to Steffen for losing my temper." I held my hand out for the koala.

Darius handed it to me and I packed it away.

"May I ask what upset you?" Darius watched me place the box in my half empty wardrobe.

"The woman who raised me died."

Darius looked uncomfortable. "I am sorry to hear that. Do you need to go home for the funeral?"

I shut my wardrobe door a little harder than necessary. "The funeral was three months ago. Apparently, my mother forgot to have me informed."

Darius's eyes hardened, his jaw tightening. "I see." He looked at the envelope on my bed with my name on it. "Is that her letter of apology?"

I laughed. "No. That is my nan's last will in testimony and a check for my inheritance."

Darius looked uncomfortable. I could tell he wanted to discuss something else, but was trying to be considerate of my emotions. I actually wanted the distraction.

"What do you really want to discuss, Darius?"

Darius hung his head a little. "That conversation tonight, about when you lost your virginity." He tilted his head to see me. "Your brother is right. That man took advantage of you."

I clasped my hands in front of me to prevent fidgeting. "It was my choice, Darius."

"Still..."

"No," I cut him off. "He didn't know my age, he couldn't have known it was my first time. I told him I wasn't very experienced; he probably never knew he was my first."

"You would have bled, Mora," Darius argued.

I shrugged.

Darius's jaw ticked with the tension of his frustration. He took a deep breath, did his counting in his head thing and calmed down. "Do you recall anything about him?"

Collecting the envelope from my bed, I shoved it into my work bag avoiding Darius's gaze. "The young man I went home with was a nobody, but he made me feel like a somebody for the first time in my life. I recall everything about that night. How he made me feel, what it was like to be with him." I swiped at the tear that escaped before he could notice. "Waiting for daylight wouldn't have changed anything."

"Why?" Darius stepped toward me, that keen observation studying me again.

Blowing out a breath, I finally lifted my eyes to meet his. "How many of your one-night stands have you ever wanted to see again, Darius?" Darius flinched. I nodded. "I was young, I wasn't naive."

We stood there for a moment, just looking at each other, reading each other's emotions. I looked away first. "I'll need to go see someone about this will and cash the check. Do you mind if I take some personal time?"

Darius waited another two breaths. "Take the day tomorrow. Get your personal life sorted out." He stepped past me.

"That's not what I meant. It will only take an hour." My personal phone started ringing. I picked it up, hiding the screen from view.

"Take the day anyway. Good night," Darius spoke over his shoulder before shutting the door behind him.

Taking a deep breath, I answered the phone. "Hi, Marshall."

"Alex told me about Freida. I am sorry, Mora. Is there anything I can do?"

"Actually, there is. I need a lawyer to look over the will for me and make sure it's all closed off properly."

I heard Marshall chuckle on the other end. "You do not trust your mother?"

"Not as far as I can throw her," I replied, walking to the window and looking out at the city lights. "I'm not saying she's trying to swindle me. I would just like a lawyer to look it over."

"Can you come see me tomorrow? I will have my lawyer look at it for you over lunch."

"I can. I'll be at your office by twelve."

"I will organize it now."

I took a deep breath. Was five years too late? "Marshall. I want to hear your side of the story."

There was silence for a moment. "I will have Tabitha clear my calendar for the afternoon. We can do the lawyer thing at lunch, talk all you need for the afternoon, and, if you are still talking to me, we can have dinner with Alex after."

I nodded, then remembered he couldn't see me. "Thank you."

Chapter Seven

I couldn't sleep. Around two in the morning I made my way down to the kitchen for a hot milk. I really wanted to play the cello, but thought my house mates might not appreciate it. I was stirring the honey into the warmed milk when Darius fit himself into the doorway.

"Trouble sleeping?" he asked. His eyes looked me over. I wasn't wearing much. Just an oversized shirt and panties. Of course, he was still in his jeans but with just that body hugging shirt.

"Shouldn't you be asleep?" I asked focusing on stirring my milk instead of his body.

"I was working."

"On what?" Work was a safe topic.

"My mentor has a charity event every year on Halloween. I have been running the event since I started Lynwood. It is the one event I still take care of every detail for personally."

I gave him a quiet smile. "Let me guess, masquerade?" I drank my milk.

"You have something against masked balls?"

"No. I love them. The chance to be anyone else for a night." I lifted my eyes and stretched out my neck. "The freedom of anonymity appeals to everyone."

Darius watched me rinse my mug and put it in the dishwasher. "Would you like to sit and talk with me until you fall asleep?"

I smirked. "What makes you think talking with you would put me to sleep?"

Darius smiled. "I can be very boring." He held out his hand to me.

I sucked in a breath of courage and took his hand. He didn't lead me to his study as I expected, but to his bedroom. He opened the heavy wooden doors, waited for me to pass, and closed them after us. The corridor leading forward was lined with what I took to be wardrobe doors. The door at the end of the corridor was open and the tiled floor and wall indicated that was his bathroom.

Darius walked forward two meters and opened a door on his left, leading me into his bedroom. The bed backed onto the corridor wall, bedside table on either side, door at the opposite side to reach the bathroom faster. There was a large window opposite the bed, a pop-up television cabinet at the foot of the bed, and that was it for furniture.

I stopped. "I don't think this is the place for talking, boss." I didn't use his name so I could pointedly remind him of our relationship.

"You need to sleep, I am ready to sleep. I believe, after the shock you suffered today, you need comforting. I respect your boundaries, Mora. We will sleep, nothing more."

Shaking my head, I started backing out of the room. Darius caught my face in his hands.

"Trust me, Mora. You need this." He pulled me into his arms and hugged me. It wasn't sexual, his hands held my upper back and the back of my head. It felt so nice being held by those strong arms, so safe and protected. I felt like I belonged in those arms. He held me to him tight until I relaxed into him. Then Darius eased his grip but continued to hold me a little longer.

Pulling back Darius looked down into my eyes, his hazel eyes soft with emotion. "Now get into bed, Miss Ellis, and I'll hold you while you sleep."

He stepped away, pulling back the covers on his bed and holding them till I complied. To say I felt uncomfortable climbing into my boss's bed would be an understatement.

"Just to clarify. This isn't considered breaking your rule about sleeping with guys under your roof?" I asked as Darius lifted his shirt over his head revealing his torso to me. My body reacted immediately. Nope, this was not a good idea.

Darius didn't smirk like I expected. He unbuttoned his jeans, casually pushing them down before kicking the pile of clothes to the side. I thanked the gods he wore boxer briefs.

"To clarify," Darius climbed into the bed beside me, pulling the covers over us before hitting a button beside the bed which turned out the lights, "the only man you are permitted to sleep with under my roof, or at work, is me."

He pulled me into his arms, and for one heart-stopping moment I thought he was going to kiss me again. His breath rattled out of his chest as if he was straining himself, his arms tensed around me. This was hard for him, he was struggling in allowing me into his bed. Resting my hand on his muscled chest, I tilted my head back to try and see his face in the dark.

"This isn't going to work, Darius. We are both tense and uncomfortable trying to force this. I should go back to my room." I pushed on his chest, his arms tightened like a boa constrictor.

"Stay. I'll relax as soon as you do." His breath breezed across the top of my head. "What would make you feel more comfortable? How do you normally sleep with your boyfriend?"

"Naked," I answered automatically. Tensing. I backtracked. "Not that I'm suggesting we get naked, I just..."

"What position, Mora?" Darius growled with a deep voice that sent my pelvic muscles into a spasm.

I took several deep breaths to calm myself, both my hormones and my anxiety. Darius waited patiently.

"Lie on your back."

Darius released his hold and rolled onto his back, his arm still under my neck. I molded my body to his side, placed my head in the nook of his shoulder and my hand above his heart. Closing my eyes, I took a few more deep breaths, telling myself it was Jasper I was lying next to. My body started to relax. As soon as I did, so did the body I was lying on.

I woke in the morning by myself. Checking the clock beside the bed, I saw it was already after eight. Normally, I was in the office by now. Darius usually went running and to the gym in the morning. He showed up at the office with the brothers before nine.

Sitting up in the bed, I looked around Darius's room. The emotions hit me like I'd been punched in the stomach. Curling over myself, I started crying. This couldn't be happening. I'd been so sure I could keep things professional between Darius and me. I wouldn't have taken the job otherwise. Last night crossed a line.

After several minutes of purging the guilt I felt, I pulled myself together and climbed out of my boss's bed. On the bonus side, everyone would be at work, so I could get back to my room with no one knowing what happened. Everyone, that is, except Steffen. He was in the kitchen as I walked past.

"Miss Ellis," he called. "Would you like some breakfast?" His voice was tense and I wasn't greeted with the customary 'good morning'.

With a deep breath I stepped into the kitchen. Steffen stopped to look at me. I imagined it was the look he gave his daughters when they did the walk of shame in their older years. It broke me. I started crying again.

"Steffen. I've made a huge mistake."

He nodded. "I know, Miss Ellis. You should never have taken the job."

***

"Everything looks in order with the financial side of things, Miss Ellis. I will chase up the deeds to the property for you. They should have been included with everything else, but it could be the bank are holding them until you tell them where you would like them sent." John Hicks explained. The former supreme justice was forced to stand down after an infidelity scandal. Now, he was my father's attorney, the one who knew I was Marshall's biological daughter.

"Thank you, John." Marshall Blake shook his hand and the lawyer left the table.

There was no denying Marshall was my father. The black hair, the pale blue eyes, and pale skin. Thankfully, I didn't have his square jaw. Alex, however, was a replica of Marshall. The genetics were obviously very strong.

We were seated in Gordon Ramsay's restaurant in London, not far from Marshall's home in Flood Street. I sat back throwing my napkin on the table. Marshall looked at me.

"She's kept the property, perhaps already transferred the deeds to her name," he explained as he took a drink of water. "What do you want to do?"

"Let her keep it." I picked up my own water. I was pretty sure my headache had nothing to do with the amount of wine I drank last night, but where I slept.

"You do not intend on going back there to live?" Marshall queried. He signaled a waiter for the bill.

"No."

"Okay, we will let her keep it, but she will pay you for it. That property must be worth a few million." Marshall signed the bill the waiter brought him.

"I already have the inheritance." I dismissed. I'd cashed the check before meeting my father at his office.

"So how does it feel to be a millionaire?" Marshall smirked at me.

"Not quite a millionaire. I feel the same as I did yesterday with only $20,000 in the bank." I took a couple of Panadol hoping to cure the thumping in my head.

"When you get the money for your grandmother's waterfront property, you will be a millionaire," Marshall smiled. "At which point, I would like you to reconsider working for me."

"Marshall." We'd been having this argument for a year.

He held up his hand. "You wanted to make your own way in the world, just like Alex did. I understood. I did the same. This will not be about the money now. One day you will have a fifty percent share in my business with your brother. I think it is time you both came on board and started earning your staff's respect."

I shook my head. "Blake Industries will be Alex's inheritance. He's worked toward proving himself good enough to follow in your footsteps. I'm happy in the job I do. I don't want to be someone's boss."

Marshall tapped the table. "You want to spend the rest of your life as an executive assistant?"

Well there you go. Alex didn't tell Marshall everything. He didn't know I was working as a personal assistant now.

"No. Eventually, I want to get married, have a few brats just like me, be a good mother and wife, and work hours that enable me to be home for my kids after school," I revealed.

Marshall raised a brow. "I didn't know that. I never expected those career aspirations from Liza Ellis's daughter."

"Did you expect them from yours?" I countered.

Marshall smiled gently. "I never gave much thought to what a daughter of mine would do. I believe all I ever hoped for, was for you to be a good person and nothing like your mother. You have not disappointed me."

"Well then, we have the same aspirations for my future. My plan is to be the exact opposite of my mother." I set my glass of water down after another mouthful. "Speaking of which. I believe you were going to give me your side of the story?"

"Yes, but not here." Marshall put his napkin on the table and stood.

A waiter pulled out my chair as I started to stand. Nodding my thanks, I followed my father out the restaurant. We walked quietly until we entered Physic Garden.

"Your mother interned for Blake Industries as a grad student. At first, I would just see her around the office while consulting with my managers, but then she kept turning up in the pub I frequented after work. Soon enough, we were sleeping together. Never at work, but she was at my place more regularly than not afterwards," Marshall started.

"It certainly was not love for either of us. Once we were done in the bedroom, we barely had anything to talk about. After several weeks, Liza started talking about her degree finishing, and how she would need to return to Australia unless she could find a job here."

Marshall looked out over the park. "I wrote her a glowing

reference to aid her in getting a good entry level role. That's not what your mother expected."

"She expected you to give her a good role in your company?"

"Yes." Marshall slipped his hands into his pockets. "Liza wanted a manager's role." He turned his topaz blue eyes to my matching ones. "I did not become the director of a fortune five hundred company by making stupid decisions. Liza was fun, she was not a commitment. I realized in that moment she was a risk to my business."

"So, you showed her the door."

"Yes. She was not happy." Marshall looked ahead again. "That was the last I heard from, or anything about, Liza Ellis, until six years later."

"Freida contacted you?"

"My personal assistant received a call from directory telling her a Freida Ellis was on the line and that it was very important. Your grandmother was very lucky I was in a good mood that day. I had actually forgotten Liza's surname and did not even connect the two. Then I got on the line and Freida kindly explained she was Liza's mother, and that our daughter was currently in hospital fighting for her life. She thought I should at least know you exist before you died."

"That must have been a shock?" I kept my eyes on the path in front of me. We were circling the park.

"It was. Knowing Liza, I expected had she bore me a child she would have come after me for everything. I asked for confirmation. Freida emailed me a copy of your birth certificate and a photo. I was named as your father, but it was the photo that convinced me. You are the spitting image of my mother, Mora. There was no denying the connection."

He smiled at me. "I was on a plane within an hour, and by your bedside thirty hours later. You were badly injured and unconscious. The doctors did not think you would make it, and, if you did, they believed you would never walk again.

"I could not believe all that damage was done by a tumble down the stairs. I confronted Freida, who was there with you, and that is when I found out you were home alone when it happened. You were six and your mother left you alone. I could not believe it."

"Who told you that crock?" I looked at him, disgusted.

Marshall looked shocked. "Freida told me your mother called her and told her she got called out for work and could she go check on you. Is that not what happened?"

"No," I tempered my response. "Liza was there that day. She was busy with her boyfriend at the time. I had to feed myself and cut my finger trying to butter my toast. I went to show her and get a band aid and walked in on them naked.

"She started yelling at me. She dragged me out of her room and threw me. I slid across the timber floor and then down the stairs. When they saw me lying at the bottom of the stairs they freaked, grabbed their stuff and left. Nan arrived thirty minutes later and called the ambulance."

Marshall stopped walking, a mixture of pain and anger flashing in his eyes. "She left you there, broken bones, bleeding internally, and left?"

I nodded, keeping my emotions out of it. "Yes. You didn't expect her to go down for child abuse did you?"

Marshall closed his eyes. "If I had known this, I would have stood a chance of getting custody of you."

I frowned at him. "Why would you do that? You live a bachelor's life. You work just as long hours as her. How could the life you offered me been any better?"

"You would not have suffered your mother's abuse for one," Marshall replied angrily.

"I didn't after that. Nan made sure she was there every day and Liza stopped acknowledging my existence." I turned and started walking again.

"I would have liked to have been there for you, to get to know you, Mora. You are my daughter, I would have gone out of my way to be there for you."

"As I hear it, you did. I just wasn't allowed to know about it."

Marshall hung his head. "I could not believe the judge's decision. It was bad enough to deny me shared custody, but to deny me the right to even know you—my lawyer suspected there might have been some bias on the judge's part. No one could believe he gave your mother everything she requested."

I cocked my head. "It wasn't Judge Harold Grady, was it?"

Marshall stopped walking again. "How did you know?"

"That was the lover who watched her throw me down the stairs. It was his neck on the line too if he crossed her. They married just before I moved here."

Marshall gritted his teeth. "That lying, cheating..." He swallowed the rest of it. "I should have followed the decision up by having both of them investigated. John suggested it, I decided it had cost enough emotionally and moved on. Your nan allowed me to be part of your life as best I could, and eventually we introduced you to Alex, even though you never caught on to that either.

"When I got the call from Freida telling me you were on your way to London, I half hoped you had finally found out about me and decided to come and meet me. Freida quickly explained that Liza had purchased you the plane ticket and kicked you out. She asked me to look after you."

"Wait. Mum didn't call you?"

"No. I called her. I got a minute of her time. Long enough for her to call me a few foul names, tell me you were an absolute brat, too much like me, and she could not stand having you there anymore. You were my problem from here on in." Marshall rolled his eyes. "She obviously did not grow as a person with age and experience."

"So, when you showed up at the airport?"

"As soon as I knew you were coming, I had a room decorated for you and waited at the airport. You were actually only four hours behind me in landing. Tabitha had a field day decorating your room, though the time frame nearly gave her conniptions. When I told her I was taking the week to settle you in—well let us just say, I have never seen that look of shock on my assistant's face. Of course, I was back at work within two days, after you made your feelings about getting to know me clear."

"I'm sorry about that. I thought you were suffering my existence as much as Liza had. Plus, the shock of actually meeting my father. It was all a bit much with moving country with a minutes notice and the expectations of going to a world class university," I apologized sincerely.

Marshall smiled. "You know, I was quite impressed with your version of rebelling. Not every father gets to brag that his daughter rebelled against her parents by getting a full scholarship to Cambridge."

"You actually bragged about me to someone?"

"To the people who knew you existed."

"So your lawyer and accountant?" I frowned, looking away.

"And Alex, his mother, Tabitha, my parents." Marshall put his hand on my shoulder turning me to look at him. "I kept you quiet because explaining the situation was too hard, Mora. Not because I was ashamed of you."

"So why doesn't anyone know about Alex?" I found it hard to believe.

"Ah, well." Marshall returned to walking. "That was his mother's request. You see, back when Alex was born, it was Merrida's reputation on the line. Alex was given my name to carry, but, when he went to college, he chose to go by his mother's maiden name so that he did not receive preferential treatment for being my son." Marshall looked at me again. "You know, I would be happy for you to take my name and for people to know you are my daughter, Mora."

"Let's leave it as it is right now. Maybe when I'm ready to get married we can discuss that again."

Marshall frowned. "Married? Did Jasper Jones propose?"

I laughed. "No. I can't see that ever happening. I think he lost his heart a long time ago to someone else." I swallowed. "I meant the futuristic marriage, when I meet a man who can handle me."

Marshall's brows knitted. "I have to say, Mora, when it comes to you and men, I've never quite worked you out there. Everything else about you, you are so much like me, I can grasp it straight away. The men you are interested in however, are always men with commitment issues."

I frowned. "I've only dated Jasper, Marshall."

"Don't you remember? The first charity event I ever took you to, you spent the night dancing with that young entrepreneur until I told you to go home. I warned you off him, Mora, because I knew he would use you. He was young and busy sewing his seed everywhere. I did not want you getting your heart broken by him."

"Well, I didn't."

"No, you did not."

"Did he ever settle down?" I asked curious. I knew he and Marshall were close and still in contact.

My father sighed. "Alas, that man, like you, is too much like me."

"I take that as a no, then?" I waited a moment. "Maybe I should look him up? What was his name again?" I teased.

Marshall gave me a warning look. "I do not believe that would be a good idea either."

We finished the round of the park and stopped walking. Marshall looked at his watch. "Well, I have booked dinner for six. That gives us four hours. Would you like to come home and tell me all the things I missed about your childhood?"

I smiled. "How about, you show me that photo album, and I fill in the missing pieces?"

Marshall smiled and offered me his arm. Accepting it, I walked with him, a sense of belonging creeping in.

***

When I got home that night, I was dreading having to face Darius after last night. I shouldn't have worried. He didn't seek me out. The next day I was kept me so busy with errands, I barely stepped inside the office. I went to Jasper on Friday, and by Monday morning, things between Darius and I were back to purely professional behaviors and conversations.

Steffen didn't say anything about my breakdown, but I could see him watching Darius and I whenever we were in the same room at home. Another week passed and a handful of silk blouses, high-end dresses and skirt suits started appearing randomly in my wardrobe. Very feminine. Some I hated, some were wearable but not my cup of tea.

I started leaving anything that I was unlikely to wear in Darius's office wardrobe. They quickly disappeared. After the first month, the styles tapered to my tastes. Once Darius had the outfits sorted, I started finding sets of shoes. Another month of filtering later, I was quite content with my suddenly choice-ridden wardrobe.

I could understand why it happened. As a representative of Lynwood Corporation, an A grade event management company, turning up in target suits sent the wrong message to the clients. I did, however, mention to Steffen that if any random sets of underwear turned up in my room, male or female, I would install a lock on my door. The gifts of clothing stopped then and there.

After another month, I felt absolutely secure in having put my moment of weakness behind me. Back to enjoying my job, I loved my life. Darius and I found our niche for working together and everything was running smoothly.

Marshall and I were trying this father daughter relationship on for size. It was still a little rocky at times, but it was getting better. Otherwise, I was truly happy for the first time in my life.

Chapter Eight

Finishing the document I was working on, I saved it as the elevator pinged. Warren had left two hours ago, already finished for the day. We'd worked through the weekend and he was keen to escape while he could. I decided to stay back and head straight to aerial from work. Steffen stopped in front of my desk with a big smile.

"Evening, Miss Ellis."

"Evening, Steffen." I took the insulated bag he handed me.

"Thank you for calling me. When he goes into his focused mode he can forget to take care of himself."

"That's the point of having a personal assistant, Steffen. To help take care of you." I smiled, setting the food aside.

"I'll see you at home then. Good Evening, Miss Ellis."

"Good night, Steffen."

He was usually in his room for the night by the time I came home. Emailing a summary to Darius before turning off my computer, I took the insulated bag to the kitchen. Heating a plate in the microwave, I removed the container with the meal Steffen had cooked at my request. Serving up the still hot meal, I covered it with an insulated lid.

Slipping out of my shoes, I collected the food tray and picked up his dry-cleaned Peabody jacket. Walking to the side door behind Warren's desk, and, using my body to push the door open, I moved quietly up the walk. Darius was scribbling furiously on a plan on his desk. Just as he had been three hours ago. I wondered if they were still the most recent plans for the Guy Fawkes Carnival.

Hanging his jacket up in the closet, I continued into the office proper. Darius changed the rules a month ago. Now, I was allowed to enter quietly and set down any plans or documents that needed his urgent attention. I just had to do it barefoot so the noise of my shoes didn't disturb him.

Placing the food tray down on the table behind him, I lifted the lid quietly and wafted the scent toward him, then just as quietly closed it again before I started back into the wardrobe.

"Mora," Darius called softly. I stuck my head back around the corner, but he hadn't looked up. "I need you to stay back. Call A.K. and tell him to come back. I'm not happy with this and we are only a week out."

Watched him for a moment, I considered that I'd worked back every night for two weeks and given up my weekend. I loved my job and I had a good work ethic, but my stress levels were reaching an all-time high. I needed an outlet soon.

Darius paused and lifted his head to see if I was still there. "Is there something wrong?"

"I'll work back and miss my stress relief again, if, and only if, you put that pencil down and eat some dinner. You are a pain in the ass when your blood sugar drops. A.K. doesn't deserve that and I certainly won't put up with it tonight."

Darius gave me that hard look before turning back to the plan. "One weekend without getting your ass smacked can't be that hard for you to endure," he retorted unhappily.

Picking up the food tray, I placed it in front of him over the plan. Darius looked up at me surprised. "That is exactly what I mean. It's okay for you. You still had your play friends over during the week." Darius's eyebrows jumped. I laughed. "You think because I'm at the other end of the house I can't hear those women mewling. I've gone two weeks Darius. Without Aerial, without sex. Two very long, stressful weeks with no outlet."

Darius's eyes looked me up and down. He pushed the chair back from the desk and gestured to his lap. "By all means, Mora. Drape yourself across. I would not turn down the privilege of spanking you."

Giving him an incredulous look at the offer he just made, I scowled. "Jesus, you can be an asshole. Just eat. I'll call A.K. for you."

Leaving the office, I moved to my desk, picking up the phone.

"Arthur King speaking," the Welsh manager of the event planning division answered on the third ring.

"Hi, A.K. The boss needs to see you."

Arthur blew out a breath. "Damn. My meal just got served. Any chance you can stall for thirty minutes? I haven't eaten all day."

"Sure. He's eating right now anyway, so that buys you a little time."

"Thanks, Mora." Arthur hung up.

Putting the phone down, I shrugged out of my suit jacket. If Darius was without tie and jacket, I could be too. The black skirt suit and matching black silk blouse I wore today was a favorite.

Making a cup of tea, I went back in the main office door. Darius was polishing off his meal. "Did you get hold of A.K?"

"Yes. He's on his way." Setting the tea down in front of him, I lifted the food tray out of his way. "What do you need from me?"

Darius looked at the plans shaking his head. "Wave a magic wand and bring it all together for me." He rubbed at the back of his neck, grimacing.

He'd been bent over plans for four days running. It was bound to have strained his muscles. Without thinking, I placed the food tray on the back table and moved behind his seat. Sliding my hands down the back of his open collar, my thumbs pressing into the thick muscle of his shoulders, I started releasing the tension.

Darius paused for a moment in shock, then relaxed into my hands and allowed me to work his neck and shoulder muscles. When I could move his head without resistance, and his shoulders were more relaxed, I slowly removed my hands.

Darius grabbed my wrist as I went to step away. He ran his fingers over a fading bruise across the underside of my arm. "Is that from a strap?" He traced the yellow mark.

"Silk," I said. His gentle touch to that sensitive skin was making that little devil inside me do cartwheels. At least I hoped it was the devil. Darius lifted his eyes to me. "From Aerial the other week." I used my free hand to move his exploring hand from my skin back to his desk.

Darius released me, watching as I picked up the tray. "Go home, Mora. A.K. and I can handle this. You can action any outcomes tomorrow morning."

Giving him a nod, I walked past his desk. "If you're sure, boss." He didn't respond, just watched me leave. Taking the tray into the kitchen, I took two steps back from the sink to breathe deeply when I heard a knock on my desk.

Peeking around the corner, Arthur King waited there. His russet red waves hung to just below his ears. His blue eyes small in his large square face. His body just as square, but full of solid muscle that was only highlighted by his well-tailored pale gray suit.

"Thanks for stalling, you are a sweet heart. Am I right to go in?"

Swallowing my moment of lust, I picked up the phone. Darius answered immediately. "Send him in. Good night, Mora."

"Good night, boss." I hung up tilting my head at A.K. to say he could go in. "He's in a mood. Be warned."

Arthur nodded understanding. "Night, Mora."

After I finished cleaning up in the kitchen, I grabbed my gym bag and work bag and headed downstairs. I was going to work it extra hard tonight at aerial. As I reached the front door of the building my personal phone rang.

"Marshall," I answered my father.

"Evening. I didn't catch you at a bad time did I?" His deep, certain voice greeted me.

"I'm just leaving work. What's up?"

"I'd like to finalize arrangements, or more, Tabitha would like to finalize arrangements and I need to give her the details." Marshall paused for effect. "I was going to have a car pick you up for Friday, but Alex insists he will bring you to your birthday party. Are you happy with that?"

"Yes. Alex has already given me a time to be ready by."

"Good," Marshall said. I could hear a pencil scratching on the other end as he wrote it down. "Now, for Christmas. I would like to have you and your brother join your grandparents and me for lunch.”

My heart leapt. I actually liked my grandparents and they seemed to really like me. Marshall had been using it as the pull card to get me to family events since he realized nearly five years ago. He probably could have seen me more often, but Granddad Blake was from Ireland originally, and after retiring, my grandparents were either globetrotting on the Queen Mary or at their estate—I called it a castle—in Ireland.

“Just lunch?”

“What do you mean just lunch?” Marshall asked exasperated.

“As in, we arrive at twelve and leave by two so you can enjoy your day off. Or, we arrive at eleven, do family time and make our way home sometime before or after dinner?” My mother’s invitation would have been the first option. I would never have asked her if that’s what she meant. Years of experience meant I knew it. With Marshall, even after five years, I still wasn’t sure where I stood.

“The second option,” Marshall replied sternly. “I will send a car for you Christmas morning.”

“I’ve moved. I’ll send Tabitha the address I can be collected from.”

Marshall was quiet for a moment. “Alex didn’t mention you moved. When did that happen?”

“Five months ago. When I started my new job.”

“You took a new job? Where? Why didn’t you tell me?” Marshall’s voice became quiet. I knew enough to know that was his unhappy voice.

“I was head hunted by a slightly bigger company. It meant a pay rise, so I took it. Still the same job.” I avoided the question.

“Where?” Marshall asked again.

“I’m heading into the subway, Marshall, and might lose you. We can talk on Friday night.” It was a bullshit excuse and he knew it.

“Why don’t you want to tell me, Mora?” His tone was understanding, laced with displeasure.

"Because, you won't approve, and I really like my new job and home." I took a deep breath. "I don't want you interfering."

Marshall took a deep breath. "You are a grown woman. You are entitled to make your own choices."

"Thank you," I exhaled a breath I hadn't realized I'd been holding.

"I will see you Friday. Good night, Mora."

"Good night, dad." And just like that, I loved my father.

***

"Thanks for meeting me for lunch today." Jasper sighed after the waiter took our orders.

"I can't stay long. We have a major event tomorrow night and Darius is stressing," I explained, setting my phone aside after yet another interruption.

"This should not take long." Jasper gulped a mouthful of water.

Studying him, I understood the cues and sat back. "Let me make this easy on you, Jasper. You've met someone and need to stop seeing me."

Jasper's jaw dropped. "How did you know?"

"You've never asked to meet me for lunch. The bag at your feet will have my gear that I left at your place, and you're as nervous as they come." I sat forward and took his hand. "You don't need to be. We were never exclusive. I never held any designs on us becoming more than friends."

Jasper's shoulders physically relaxed as he smiled. "Whoever wins your heart is going to be a very lucky man, Mora."

I shrugged. "Do you want to tell me about her?"

"I went home for my mother's sixtieth and my ex, Penny, was there for the party." Jasper started to explain. Penny was his high school sweetheart. When he started his medical residency, she decided, she couldn't marry a doctor who wouldn't be around half the time. She married a lawyer a year later. Jasper gave up medicine and girlfriends. I was the closest he'd come to a girlfriend in ten years.

"We started talking and one thing led to another," Jasper explained. I raised a brow. Jasper laughed. "Don't look at me like that, Mora. Her divorce was finalized three months ago."

"She left you once before, Jasper," I reminded him with concern. I didn't want to see her break his heart again.

"I was working seventy-hour shifts."

"You still work late nights."

"I don't have to. I have managers to do the grunt work now." His smile grew with each of my questions.

"Any children?"

"No, but she would like some."

I took my hand back. "Will she let you bleed her?"

The smiled vanished off his face. "She is very conservative in her sexual interests."

"Will that work for you?"

"I will make it work. I have never stopped loving her, Mora." He finger-combed his hair. "I'm in the midst of buying a place halfway to Dorchester. That way I can be closer to her, and still an easy commute to work."

Bowing my head, I sat back. "Then I wish you all the best, Jasper."

Jasper studied me, the smile returning. "You really harbor no jealousy or hard feelings about this, do you?"

"I care for you, Jasper. I would consider you one of my closest friends. But you are not the man I will marry."

Jasper nodded. "Do you think that will happen, Mora? Marrying the man who stole your seventeen-year-old heart."

Yes, I'd told Jasper about that night, and for him, I'd given the truth.

My phone started ringing. Glancing at the screen, I watched Darius's profile flash like a beacon. "I don't know. I just have to wait and see I guess." I hit receive and put the phone to my ear. "Yes, boss?"

"Where are you?"

"The cafe across the road getting lunch," I replied honestly.

"Oh. Grab me a roll and get back here. I have meetings all afternoon and a dinner tonight so I am going to need you to deal with A.K. and Simon from the coordination team to make sure these changes are actioned."

"Yes, boss." As soon as Darius hung up, I waved the waiter over. "A roast lamb roll, mint, sweet potato and extra gravy to take away please. Make my chicken roll take away also please."

"Yes, Mora." The waiter rushed to the kitchen. They knew me here and who I was usually ordering for.

Giving a small shake of his head, Jasper snickered. "I hope he is worth it, Mora."

When Jasper stood, I rose to meet him, letting him pull me into a long hug. "Me too, Jasper."

Pulling back, Jasper caressed a finger down my cheek and kissed me tenderly. It was a little too passionate for a public location, but it had never stopped him before.

"Goodbye, Mora." Jasper walked out.

Taking a deep breath, I collected the bag with my stuff from the floor. I would miss Jasper, but I'd never been in love with him. Paying for our lunch, I collected the rolls I ordered, and headed back to work.

With every month that passed since Darius Rafal offered me the job, I felt the pages on chapters of my life slamming shut. A new path was opening before me. I just had to stay the course and let life lead me to where I was meant to be. Right now, that was very much in the presence of a man who was making me rethink my agnostic beliefs.

As I walked in the side entrance to Darius's office, I watched him pace back and forth behind his desk aggressively while talking on the phone. The mental image of a panther came to mind. With that top button undone, the tie loose and hanging, I could easily believe this man was an ancient god living in modern times. He gave off a primal energy that pulled at my soul. He was so gorgeous my body reacted to just the idea of his touching me.

Though, it was more than that. There was something about this man that was so familiar, as if I'd known him my entire life and woke up this morning in the wrong place. It'd been that way since the first time we met. With a deep breath, I put those thoughts out of my mind. He was my boss. Only my boss.

***

"You're up late," Darius spoke quietly from the walkway through the reception room.

It was Thursday night, one day after I'd given my boss a massage in his office. Twelve hours after Jasper confirmed my suspicions. Sprawled in front of the fire place, I lay with my laptop open, a cord running across to the corner to keep it powered. My research was spread around me like angel wings.

I held up a hand not looking at him. "Wait." I clicked the mouse. "Save and Submit." I waited for the confirmation to appear on the screen. It took a full fifteen seconds. I counted. Saving a copy of the receipt, I exhaled.

Rolling onto my back, I stretched long, held it for a good ten seconds, and then went limp. My head lolled to the side and I smiled up at Darius. He looked gorgeous as usual.

Darius stood, hands in the pockets of his suit pants, jacket open, white dress shirt open at the collar, bow tie hanging loose. He smiled and that little devil inside me started doing somersaults in my stomach.

"What's that smile for?" he asked, his eyes running over me like they so often did, making me feel naked.

I wasn't. I wore a pair of lounge pants and a singlet with inbuilt bra, but under those glazed eyes, I felt naked. I studied his eyes harder. "You've been drinking."

Darius's smile grew a little larger. He shrugged out of his jacket and sank into the reading chair by my feet. "My mentor from college and I catch up for dinner occasionally. Sometimes the drinking gets a little out of hand." Darius looked at the mess I'd made of the smaller lounge area on my bedroom's side of the fire place in the reception room. "Working on your project?"

"Yes. I just finalized it." I stayed there smiling at him. I couldn't look away.

Darius sat straighter. "Already? Did you want me to read it over for you?"

"I just submitted it. Sophie and Jasper read it through for me."

Darius's eyes lost some of their glaze at the mention of Jasper's name. When his eyes traveled over me again, I had to bite my lip when my pelvic muscles tightened in longing. I couldn't stop myself from squirming. Darius's eyes shot straight back to meet mine. Damn it. He knew exactly what my body just did.

He frowned. "How long since you have seen Mr. Jones? I noticed you have been around the last few weekends."

I thought about when I last stayed at his place. "Three weeks. Between work, getting my project done, and Jasper's trips back to Dorchester to see his family, it's been three weeks."

As soon as I admitted how long it had been, that devil inside me started causing a riot in my nether regions. Bitting my lip harder. I squeezed my thighs tight.

Darius watched me intently. "That is a long time for you to go without, isn't it?"

"You have no idea." My eyes traveled over him.

"You need to stop looking at me like that, Mora," he warned. "I have consumed enough liquor tonight to take the invitation you are giving me with those eyes."

"About that." My foot slipped under the base of his pants and rubbed the bare skin of his leg. Damn it, the devil was going to win tonight. "If I was to suck your cock right now, on the scale of one to ten—ten being I'm fired and homeless—how exactly would that affect our working relationship?"

Darius grabbed my ankle, pulling my foot free of his trouser leg. Dropping to the floor, he crawled himself over me. My breathing picked up at his proximity. I didn't dare move. Darius hovered over me. His mouth over mine. He breathed out purposefully causing me to pull back from the skank on his breath. "What have you been drinking?"

He smiled. "Cunt. Slutty cunt." Darius watched me. "Still want to suck my cock, Mora?"

I met his eyes unflinching. "That all depends. Did your cock fuck that slutty cunt?"

Darius smiled at me. After a minute, he reached over shutting my laptop. "Go to bed, Mora. Think about that guy you lost your virginity to and take care of your urges. Then tomorrow night, go see your boyfriend."

Standing up Darius grabbed his jacket from the chair. Exhaling, I rolled onto my stomach. "I won't be seeing Jasper this weekend. I have a family thing to go to." Kneeling back, I started gathering my research together, piling it on my laptop. "I can take a hint. I'll stay at Alex's for the weekend."

Darius ran his hand through his hair. "I did not mean..."

"Yes, you did." I stood up and turned to face him. "And you are right to. I shouldn't have behaved like that. I apologize." Gathering my stuff, I made my way up the stairs to my room.

After packing everything away I changed and climbed into bed. Lying there replaying what just happened downstairs, I was sure he wanted me. He all but said he did. I hadn't misheard that. Exhaling, I picked up my phone and dialed my best friend.

"Hey, hon. All ready for tomorrow night?" Sophie chirped.

"Hopefully. I've got my outfit packed in a bag and my dress packed so I can change at work." I looked to where the garment bag hung from the wardrobe door. "I submitted my project."

"Really?" Sophie squawked. "Does that mean you are finished?"

"It does. Presuming I pass."

"As if you won't. We will have to celebrate doubly tomorrow night. Did you do shots with your house mates tonight to celebrate?"

"I tried to give my boss a blow job. He turned me down."

"He what?" Sophie sounded offended. "That guy is insane. I would let you go down on me."

"I'll keep that in mind when I'm gegging for it tomorrow night."

"No, seriously, what is his damage?"

"He'd actually just come home from getting his rocks off. Plus, there is the fact that I work for him," I excused.

"That just makes you easy access, especially in his house."

"That also makes things rather more complicated than a random blow job off an employee in the mail room."

"True," Sophie sympathized. "How are things with Jasper?"

"How are things with Alex?"

"Going to be like that, are we?" Sophie grumbled. "He is still happy to have fun with me, but nothing else. I just cannot find the time for him these last couple of weeks."

"Hoping he'll realize what he's giving up?" I rolled my eyes. I couldn't see Alex being the sort of guy to be manipulated so easily.

"Just giving him a taste of his own medicine. I am sick of it always being his choice when we hook up." Sophie typed into a computer on the other side. "Speaking of which, Dean is back in the country. Do you mind if I invite him tomorrow?"

Dean was Sophie's older brother. He was twenty-six and a pilot for the air force. He liked to come out with us when he was home.

"Sure. I'll leave your names at the door. It feels like he's been away for years this time." Slipping my legs beneath the quilt, I snuggled down. "It will be good to see him."

"Yeah, it does. You going to sleep now?" Sophie knew my sleepy voice well.

"Yes."

"Okay." Sophie paused. "So, do you think your sexy boss will sneak into bed with you later?"

"Soph. Don't put that shit in my head before I sleep. I'll end up dreaming about him."

"As if you don't already." Sophie laughed. "Night, hon. And happy birthday."

Checking the clock; it was in fact past midnight. "Thanks, Soph." Setting the phone aside, I settled into bed.

At three in the morning, I woke from a dream about Darius and I that involved his office desk and his head under my skirt. Groaning, I collected my vibrator from the bedside table. Not bothering with foreplay, I was riled up from the dream already and good to go. I went fast. My back arched off the bed, free hand clawing at the sheets beneath me as I came voicelessly, pretending it was Darius pounding into me.

As I caught my breath and fell limp on the bed, I looked at the ceiling and swore. Fantasizing about the boss wasn't a good idea for my mental well-being. I lay there awake scolding myself. When next I looked at the clock it was four in the morning and I decided to get an early start to my day.

Showering, I packed my bags for the weekend, grabbed my work bag and garment bag, and headed for the front door. I learned a while ago there was no sneaking past Steffen, not even at ungodly hours in the morning.

"Good morning, Miss Ellis." Steffen already dressed, took one of my bags and handed me a thermos as I stepped into the foyer. "Hot chocolate for the ride into work."

"How do you always know, Steffen? Do you have a monitor in your room that alarms whenever I try to sneak out?"

Steffen walked to the lift ignoring my question. "I will meet you in the garage. I am on my way to the market so I will drop you at the office on the way." He pressed the elevator button, the doors opened and he stepped inside.

Turning to close the apartment door, Darius stood at the other end of the entry foyer, just his jeans pulled on, hair still messed from sleep. His eyes were hard, unreadable. I cleared my throat. "I'll see you at the office, boss."

Chapter Nine

The phone was ringing as I came out of the bathroom. I didn't have my shoes on yet, so ran to my desk and picked it up. "Darius Rafal's office."

"It's Warren. Is he nearly ready to go?"

"He should be. He was in the shower when I went to change." Checking the phone I noticed the line in his office lit up. "He's on the phone."

"Get him off. The car is about to pull up out front. This is the one event each year he insists on overseeing himself. He cannot run late."

"Where are you?" I asked slipping into my shoes.

"I was held up. I am closer to home now so I will change there and meet him at the event." Warren paused. "Are you sure you will not ditch the family thing and come? It is a pretty great evening."

Warren asked me to be his date for the event. "Sorry, Warren. Family first. We are going to Hesitate to party tonight if you want to join us after."

"That sounds good. Text me when you are on your way and we will meet you there."

"Good. I'll go round our boss up."

"Thanks, Mora. Have a good night."

"You too." Hanging up, I walked through the side door into Darius's office. He stood at his desk on the phone, still only half-dressed. "Shit."

From the wardrobe, I grabbed the emerald green shirt and black tie he'd chosen for the night and moved into his office. Since I'd started working for him, I'd seen Darius once without his shirt before today. The night I'd slept in his arms. Now, I'd seen him half-dressed twice in one day.

Darius turned to face me as I walked toward him holding out the shirt for him to slip into. With a glance at the clock he turned, sliding his arms in. When he faced toward me, I fastened the buttons.

Without blinking, I unzipped his fly and tucked his shirt in before zipping him back up. I ignored when my hand brushed his junk, twice. Threading the tie around his neck, I popped his collar and tied a tidy knot before setting his collar right. All while avoiding eye contact.

Moving into the wardrobe, I came back with his shoes and socks. With a hand on his chest, I pushed him down into his chair. He sat; I knelt and slipped his socks on. When I picked up the first shoe, I glanced up. Darius was watching me with wide eyes. Dropping my gaze, I slipped his feet into his shoes, tying the laces for him.

Trying very hard to read nothing into this, I couldn't deny there was something highly erotic about dressing this man. I would be lying if I said I tied those laces as fast as possible. I didn't. Taking my time, I enjoyed the heat of his gaze on me.

Once finished, I stood and fetched his jacket and cuff links from his wardrobe. By the time I stepped back into the office proper, Darius was off the phone. Holding his jacket for him, he slid it on.

"Your car is waiting downstairs. You are now officially late." I handed him the cuff links. "Do the rest in the car on the way."

Turning to look at me, his hand slid along my neck, and palmed my face. With wide eyes I held my breath as his face descended. He kissed my cheek. "Thank you, Mora. Enjoy your weekend." Grabbing his tablet, Darius walked out the door, grabbing his thicker winter jacket from the coat rack as he passed.

With a deep breath, I locked out his computer and shut the office up for the weekend. When the elevator pinged, I grabbed up my bags. Alex materialized at my desk with a broad grin and a small birthday present.

"Happy birthday, Mora." He handed me a present. Smiling, I pulled him into a hug. "You will have to open it in the car. We do not want to keep Marshall waiting."

"Thanks, Alex."

Alex took my bag and frowned. "What's the bag for?"

"Do you mind if I crash at your pad for the weekend?"

"You're not staying with Jasper?" Alex asked pushing open the door to the stairs.

"No. We aren't seeing each other anymore," I confided.

Alex looked astounded. "What happened?"

"He's met someone else. He's in the midst of moving out of London so he can be closer to her and still have a reasonable commute to work each day."

Entering the foyer, we found Zander standing by the front doors. Zander's eyes popped open when he saw me. The off-the-shoulder bodice of my dress was stretch-black velvet, the skirt was a river of black silk. There was a belt of black lace sewn around the join of skirt and bodice which matched the soft lace of the long sleeves. It definitely cost more than a week's pay, but I could afford it now.

"You look stunning." Zander smiled brightly. His eyes fell on the birthday present I was carrying. "Is it a birthday party you are going too?"

"Yes, Zander." I smiled shyly.

Peering down at the gift Zander saw my name on the envelope. He frowned. "It is your birthday?"

"Yes, Zander. Good night."

Alex held the door for me and I followed him out to the waiting car. He waited till we were safely in the car before looking back at Zander. Following his gaze, I saw Zander on the phone.

"They did not know it was your birthday?" Alex asked carefully.

"They've got a major event on tonight. They were too busy to notice."

Alex took my hand in his. "What is going on, Mora? You have your walls up."

Looking up to my big brother, I sighed. "I actually don't know, Alex." Taking a deep breath, I forced a smile. "But, I do know it's my twenty-third birthday, Halloween, and that I submitted my final project last night."

Alex smiled. "Congratulations, Mora. Looks like we have a lot to celebrate tonight."

"Leila isn't coming, is she?"

Alex's eyes popped. "God, no. I'm not putting her anywhere near Marshall. Why?"

"Because Sophie will be here tonight."

"Mora..." Alex started to growl.

"Not what you think, bad wolf." I pretend smacked his nose. "You know we do aerial together." Alex nodded. "Well, this year she's one of the performers. So, she will be at the event and then will join us at Hesitate afterwards."

Alex took a deep breath. "She is not returning my calls right now."

"I know. She's stepping aside, Alex. She was never the mistress type. It's time she gave you up and focused on finding someone who can make her the primary in his life."

Alex sighed. "I've heard this happens to women around this age. Is that what is happening with you and Jasper?"

Squeezing his hand, I let him go. "He's had two years of me, Alex. It's time to move on for both of us."

The car pulled up at the event. A valet opened the door and Alex slid out before turning and giving me his hand. Once on the side walk, the valet shut the door and the car pulled away. Alex took my arm in his and escorted me up the roped off entranceway. Photographers on either side took photos of the guests arriving, hoping to catch a celebrity or someone equally important. No one really wanted to know about us which I was happy about.

"You know. If they take our photo and put it on the social pages, Leila will flip her lid."

"She will flip her lid if she knows you stayed at my place this weekend," he whispered back.

I looked at him worried. "I can stay at Dad's or Sophie's."

Alex patted my hand. "Would you mind? I don't need any more girl trouble right now."

"Of course, I don't. I totally forgot about Leila when I asked. Don't worry about it."

We stepped inside where we were by Arthur King who was marking off the guest list. "Mora, I did not realize you were someone who would have her own personal invite to this event." A.K. looked at the invitation I handed him then Alex's and frowned at the list. "We're here for a private event upstairs."

"Oh, I didn't realise there was another event on tonight." He frowned. I understood why. Now guests from the other event would also be clotting up his red carpet.

"Yes. I believe we are included in your list as a group so that we can join the event later. Our names should be on the extras list. Sophie and Dean Trent are also there."

Arthur checked the list for staff, performers, and other important, but not necessarily invited guests. Smiling when he saw the names, Arthur stepped aside. "Excellent. Thanks, Mora. Have a good night."

"You too, A.K."

We moved farther in to where our jackets were taken. "How the hell did you pull that off at the last minute?" Alex chuckled. "I didn't even know Dean was back."

"Neither did I till last night. Luckily, I am in the beneficial position of having access to the guest list."

Alex laughed holding up his wolf mask that would cover the upper two thirds of his face when he put it on. I held mine up. We wouldn't wear them till we came back downstairs for the ball. Alex tilted his head.

"A black owl?"

"Also known as the greater sooty owl. They only reside along the east coast of Australia." It was tradition for me to chose an Australian animal and teach Alex a little more about Australia.

"Owl's hunt mice and snakes correct?" Alex lifted a brow.

I smiled as he led me into the antechamber. "Most do yes. The greater sooty owl is a powerful hunter and prefers much larger prey."

"Is that so?" Alex smiled. "You like to pick significant animals to your situation, don't you?"

Tilting my head, I batted my lashes. "I'm not sure what you mean, Mr. Hark?"

Rolling his eyes, I chuckled and Alex's smile grew. "Marshall is over there."

Following his gaze, I grabbed his arm before he could step forward. "Wait. We can't go over there yet."

Alex frowned then finally recognized Marshall was talking to Darius. "It is only your boss."

I stepped us back a bit. "Yes. My boss, who knows we are siblings and that my father is a very powerful business man. Put us side by side and what do you think he's going to see, Alex?"

Alex assessed me, noting the dark hair, pale skin, and topaz eyes of my father. He swore under his breath. "Okay. I will get Tabitha's eye and we will meet him in the room upstairs."

Moving us to the roped off staircase, we showed the guard there our invitations for the private event being held upstairs. The guard nodded opening the rope for us to step through. Once we were halfway up the stairs, Alex waved to Tabitha.

Spotting us almost immediately, Tabitha tucked a strand of her golden curls behind her ear as she whispered to Marshall. Glancing in our direction, Marshall nodded once before returning to his conversation. Gesturing he was moving to Darius, they turned to talk and walk. Darius's eyes seized upon the two black clad figures on the stairs, his lips faltering in the conversation.

He'd seen me in my dress. I didn't think he'd taken that much notice, but apparently, he had. Turning away from him, I started up the stairs. "Damn it. He saw us."

Alex put his arm on my lower back as we walked. "He is very observant, but with you he pays very special attention. I saw it the night on the terrace at his house."

"He can't figure me out. It bothers him," I shrugged it off.

Alex smirked. "It bothers everyone, Mora. One day, you will have to let someone inside that fortress you have locked yourself away in."

"I let you in."

Alex rubbed my back. "I am inside the fortress, I am still locked out of the tower."

When we reached the top of the steps, Alex led us to a small room. There was a waiter there and he showed us to a table that held some finger foods and a beautifully decorated birthday cake.

"Do you like it?" Tabitha came in, a large smile on her face.

"I do." I smiled back. "The company throwing this gig doesn't know about this right?"

Tabitha shook her head as if I was being silly. "Of course not. I organized this with the function center myself." She looked at her watch. "Marshall should be up in a second. He went through to the back steps to come up. There are not many people here yet, so you two were very conspicuous going up those stairs."

The door opened as a laughing old couple came through the door. The elderly woman took one look at us and a grin burst across her face. "There are my wonderful grandchildren." Enid Blake swept forward and bundled me up in a hug. "Happy birthday, Mora."

I hugged her back. "Thank you, Nanna."

Enid stepped back and gave Alex a hug. Granddad Blake gave me a bear hug before shaking hands with Alex.

"Looks like I'm last as always." Marshall came in, shutting the door. He walked straight to me and gave me the biggest hug. "Happy birthday, sweetheart."

"Thanks, dad," I murmured in his embrace.

***

"You have fun tonight," Marshall murmured as we left the private function room. He turned toward the back of the building and disappeared with Tabitha.

Our grandparents walked with Alex and I. "Arthur and I just booked a three-month cruise on the Queen Mary Two over our winter. It will take us to Australia, Mora." Enid smiled. "I was saying to Arthur, we should do a holiday in Australia one year and take you with us as our tour guide."

I forced a smile. "That's a lovely idea, Nanna, but I've barely seen any of Australia. Alex has probably seen more than me."

"So, you could see it with us," Enid pressed.

"Maybe one year, Nanna."

Enid shook her head. "You are just as bad as Alex. So keen to make your mark in the world, you miss out on all the fun of being young."

"I'm quite happy to leave this world without anyone, but the people I love, knowing my name, Nanna. A career as a personal assistant does not generally lead to fame."

"Unless you are diddling your high-profile boss and the media finds out about it. Right, Nanna?" Alex winked.

Enid blushed and I swear I'd missed some story there.

"Behind every great man is an even greater woman," Arthur smirked.

I didn't understand the jest. Arthur and Enid were working class for most of their lives, quite often barely making ends meet. My father was a self-made billionaire. One of those genius young entrepreneurs who take the world by storm. New money, as some would call him. With that new money, he'd raised his father's simple engineering business to be a national name with government contracts. It set Arthur and Enid up for life.

"Who are you working for now, my dear?" Enid queried.

"I'm in the entertainment industry now, Nanna. Just a lowly personal assistant to the faceless man behind the talent," I dodged.

Everyone put on their masks and we descended the stairs to join the much larger crowd filing into the function center. Alex took my arm. "I'm going to steal the first dance with the birthday girl if you don't mind." Alex smiled before kissing our grandparents' cheeks. We knew the drill. Family happened behind closed doors.

It was strange, because that wasn't Marshall's request. Alex wanted to make his own way in the business world without the stigma of being Marshall Blake's son. I'd elected to fly under the radar because I preferred to remain anonymous.

Stealing me away into the crowd, Alex held my hand and took me out onto the dance floor. We stepped into each other and started waltzing with the rest of the dancers on the floor. We'd been each other's dance partners at every one of our father's events since I moved here. Alex learned to dance professionally growing up. Marshall insisted. I just followed Alex's lead. By the fifth song we were both starting to sweat.

"I think we need drinks." Alex chuckled when his grip on my hand slipped.

"Agreed." I happily stopped dancing. "We should find Sophie and Dean."

Alex hesitated. "Or we could not."

I glared at Alex. "You knew she was my friend when you started screwing around with her, Alex. Just because your cake isn't as sweet anymore isn't my fault. It's my birthday, suck it up."

"Ouch." Alex pulled away as if I'd bitten him. A huge smile on his face. "Fine, I will 'suck *it* up', just for you." He winked.

I rolled my eyes. "Those details I don't need to hear."

Alex chuckled as we reached the bar. "Shots?"

"Just water for now. Unless you want to see me fall and break my neck tonight?"

"A water and a scotch." Alex smiled at the barman before turning back to me. "Does your boss know he's paying you twice over?"

"No. And with any luck, he won't even know it's me up there." I tapped my face mask.

Alex smiled, then his smile dropped as strong arms wrapped around my waist and a scruffy mouth kissed my neck. "There you are," Zander spoke in my ear.

I turned to face him. He wore a midnight blue mask with his navy-blue suit and silver shirt. Warren stood behind him in exactly the same outfit. They could have been twins.

Zander held up a small parcel. "Happy birthday, Mora."

Accepting the present with a shy smile, I unwrapped it. Inside was a gift card to the place Darius and the brothers regularly attended for massages. I raised an eyebrow. "Any chance they give happy endings?" Yes, I was definitely riled up after last night.

Zander's head tilted surprised. "Not this place, but I know a few private masseuses who would definitely help you out there."

Remembering they weren't aware I wasn't seeing Jasper anymore, I forced a wicked smile and winked. Zander relaxed and smiled back. Slipping the voucher into my clutch, I left the wrapping on the bar.

Warren shoved his brother out of the way handing me an envelope with his charismatic smile. "You should have told us it was your birthday. Getting presents at the last-minute means calling in favors."

Opening the envelope to find a gift voucher for a high-end lingerie store, I barely swallowed my surprise. "Guys, this is too much."

"Nonsense. We adore you," Zander reassured.

"And while I am aware you have some nice lace scanties," Warren winked using my own description from five months ago, "I figure buying something ultra-sexy and naughty for your birthday is a must do for women."

Alex handed me my drink after I slipped the voucher in my clutch. "Considering your boss has declared her hands off, do you really think it is appropriate to be buying my little sister, who is more than ten years younger than you, sexy, naughty lingerie?" Alex queried with warning.

Warren gave Alex his naughty smile. "The boss said hands off. He never said I could not look or fantasize about her." Warren stepped closer to me, his height towering over me. He had a few inches on Alex. "Have you seen your sister's idea of sleepwear? I cannot tell you how many nights that has sent me off to bed with a smile."

Slipping an arm around my waist, Warren pulled me into a very open-mouthed kiss. I melted into him. Surprised when I took the kiss a little further by adding tongue to it, Warren stepped back.

The smile was gone and he looked somewhat flushed as he cleared his throat. "Well—happy birthday, Mora." He took two quick steps back from me.

"Thank you. And thank you for the lovely presents. I'll be sure to show you what I buy," I winked at Warren. He sucked in a deep breath.

"Cool it, Mora. I think Warren likes his job too much to risk losing it to relieve you of your monthlong dry spell," Alex warned.

"Monthlong dry spell?" Zander queried.

"Jasper's and my schedule haven't been syncing a lot of late."

Warren collected drinks from the bar for him and Zander. "And he's not here this weekend again?"

"Nope." Taking Alex's hand, I checked his watch. "I've got to go find Sophie. I'll find you after."

"Sure. Be safe and I want at least one more waltz before we bail." Alex gave me a concerned look.

"I would like a dance too." Zander stopped me walking off.

"If you can find me, you can dance with me." I winked as I merged into the crowd.

Heading for the stage where the musicians were set up, I then made my way around to the side and the backstage area. The security guard posted there stopped me, but let me through when I explained I was one of the performers. Sophie was already out the back changing when I walked in and removed my mask.

"There you are. I was about to send out a search party," she teased, throwing a bag at me.

"Got held up with birthday wishes."

"Well, you have to wait till later to get my present. It was too big to bring tonight. Dean has it in his car."

"You didn't have to get me anything." Birthday presents, while I loved them, made me uncomfortable.

Sophie gave me an ungracious look and continued to change into her glamorous leotard dress. It was a match to mine. Ocean blue in color, the top was designed to look like a formal dress, the skirt was sheer allowing the leotard to be visible beneath. It was elegant but still allowed for flowing movement, the splits up the side enabling us not to get our legs caught in the fabric.

Gliding on my skin-colored footless stockings, I then stepped into the dress. Sophie's hair was already braided so she quickly braided mine for me. Handing her the matching masks, we stood taking deep breaths to calm our nerves.

"You good?" I asked, squeezing her hand. Sophie was always very anxious before taking the stage.

Sophie laughed. "You have asked me the same thing for the last five years before every performance. Of course, I'm good."

A.K. knocked on the door. "When you are ready."

Sophie opened the door. "We are ready."

A.K. nodded and led the way, moving to signal the musicians as he did. The lights in the ballroom dimmed. Sophie and I took our places in front of the stage. An area cleared already by the event management. I gave Sophie's hand one last squeeze and stepped away.

The music started and the lights gave a slight glow around us. We waited for the first lyrics of the song, then started our choreographed dance. A hush went over the guests. Sophie and I had been practicing this routine for nearly a year since Lynwood had contacted our aerial school for performers for tonight.

As the first verse ended, Sophie and I started climbing the silks hanging from the ceiling. We moved in perfect unison, using the beat of the music to keep us in time. We climbed and hung, wrapped and fell our way through the music. We flew, and as I did, I forgot about the crowd below. This was my freedom. When I was up in the silks the world stopped existing for me.

As the performance came to an end, I wrapped the silk around me as we'd practiced. The final chords of the music began to play and we fell, tumbling out of the heavens like falling angels. My mask hit the silk through the fall and it was knocked from my head. I finished hanging limp from the silk as planned, not concerned with the loss of mask.

Sophie and I returned to Earth and as the lights returned to normal. Darius stood front and center, his eyes trained on me. The look on his face was unreadable. I couldn't tell if he was angry, or impressed. He was a stone carving, only his eyes moving, tracking me as I moved to the backstage area.

Sophie took my hand collecting my attention. "I think you are busted," she whispered with a laugh.

"I guess so."

Sophie nudged me with her shoulder as we entered the change room. "Maybe he will put you over his knee."

I gaped at Sophie. "He's my boss."

Sophie gave me a knowing look. "Uh-huh. And that stopped you last night. I get the shower first."

Groaning, I slapped my forehead. Sometimes confiding in your friends was not a good idea.

***

Sophie was dressed by the time I came out of the shower.

"Dean's waiting outside the door." Sophie smiled. "Alex is there too."

Oh, I knew that smile. Without a doubt, Sophie planned to be going home with my brother tonight. I guess I wasn't the only person needing a good...

There was a knock at the door. "I'm coming in," Dean warned.

Thankfully, I was in my underwear when the door swung open and Sophie's brother stepped into the room, followed closely by my brother. Dean's brown eyes glanced over me and the smile on his face spread.

"Do I have timing or what?" Dean pulled me into his arms and kissed me. It was chaste, just lips pressed to each other. "Happy birthday, baby."

"That is my sister you are drooling on," Alex grumbled.

"And my future wife." He'd been telling me since Sophie introduced us when I was eighteen we were going to marry one day, yet the most he'd ever done was kiss me. Not passionately. Just lips pressing. Dean turned to Alex. "Like you can talk, Hark. You've been boning my sister for nearly a year. When are you going to make an honest woman out of her?"

Alex and Sophie instantly became the uncomfortable couple in the room.

"Yeah, that's what I thought," Dean growled. He turned those puppy-dog eyes back to me. "Get dressed, baby. I plan to get you drunk enough to marry me tonight."

Shaking my head with a smile, I pulled my dress formal dress back on. Dean zipped me up. I let my hair out, a slight wave through it from the braid.

Taking her brother's hand, Sophie opened the door. "We'll meet you outside." She gave Dean a feral look as they left. "I cannot believe you said that. You know he has a girlfriend."

"I cannot believe you'd get involved with him, since *you* know he has a girlfriend," Dean retorted.

"Says the guy with a girl in every port and making moves on another guy's girl." Sophie shut the door after them.

Alex shook his head, handing me my owl mask. "Please be careful with Dean tonight, Mora. I do not believe he is joking about marrying you."

I laughed. "I know he is, Alex, and that is all that matters."

"If you are sure."

"Oh, trust me. I've been drunk in Dean's house often enough that if he wanted to make a move, he would have done so by now."

Alex raised an eyebrow at me, but left it alone as we moved out to the ballroom where Alex took my hand. "Last dance, then we can start your birthday party."

Twirling me under his arm as we stepped onto the dance floor, Alex moved us straight into a dance. I didn't know what it was, but it wasn't a waltz. It was like walking in line, but changing who was walking backwards every couple of steps.

"You looked amazing up there," Alex praised as we danced. "Dad was in awe watching you. I think he nearly ruined his pants when you let go and dropped to hang upside down like you did."

"It was good to perform and know he was there." I smiled. "All those years I never knew he was watching. It's nice to know."

Alex's hands gave me a gentle squeeze. "Do not look now, Mora, but I think you are starting to let those walls down."

"Shh. Don't tell me. Just let them crumble and be prepared to carry my lifeless body from the rubble if it all goes to hell."

Alex shook his head. He got the joke. He just didn't like it.

"May I cut in?" Darius tapped Alex on the shoulder.

"Sure. Just get her to the door by eleven or she will turn into a pumpkin." Looking unimpressed, Alex turned back to me. "I will find Sophie and Dean and then we can get going."

With a nod to Alex, I stepped into Darius's waiting arms. He started us into a clumsy waltz. He was still a good dancer, but after dancing with Alex, it just wasn't as professional. Darius did, however, hold our lower bodies a little tighter to each other, causing me to arch my back more to keep our bodies apart.

"You told me you were at a family function tonight," he started quietly.

"You saw me walking up the stairs where my family had a private function room booked," I replied evenly.

"I checked at the door, Mora. Your name was on the extras list."

I met Darius's eyes through my mask. "If you checked the list for the past few years, you would find my name there, Mr. Rafal. Attendance at this ball is an annual affair for my family." Darius looked at me as if he didn't believe me. Sighing, I stepped back from him. "My friends are waiting for me."

Picking up my hand, Darius moved us back into the dance. "Warren asked you to be his date. You could have said yes. That you did not makes me think you are hiding something, Mora."

"Alex is my date tonight. He is every year. We don't bring our lovers near our family," I responded with strained patience.

"And why is that?"

"Jesus!" I breathed in exasperation. "Have you even heard of boundaries? I'm not working for you tonight. You don't get to control me."

"Technically, you are working for me tonight, albeit as a performer instead of my personal assistant."

"Mr. Rafal, is there any chance we could just dance and not fight?" I seethed.

Brows lifted in surprise, Darius shut his mouth and pulled me tight to him, our bodies moving against each other, his mouth at my cheek. "You looked amazing on those tissu tonight," he praised quietly, using the French term for silks. "You took my breath away."

"You didn't even know it was me." I rolled my eyes.

"Didn't I?"

His eyes shined bright with hidden knowledge when I met them. He was maskless, and I could easily see when his eyes flicked to my lips. We hovered there, lips only inches apart, then his face moved closer and I knew he was going to kiss me.

I wanted to kiss him. I wanted to do more than kiss him. I wanted to love this man. I wanted him. In that moment, I closed my eyes and hated he was my boss. Shying my face away, his lips landed just to the side of my mouth.

"Excuse me." Dean stepped up next to us, placing his hand in the small of my back. "I have to steal the birthday girl away. We have a night of frivolity ahead of us and need to get started early."

Darius stepped back, surprise flashing before he noticed Dean's body pressed up beside mine, pulling me into him.

Anger washed over Darius's features. "Of course," Darius growled and walked away into the crowd.

Dean watched, slightly amused by Darius's reaction. "Did I interrupt something?"

"No," I grumbled. "Let's go get plastered."

Dean walked me to find the others, shrugging off whatever he just interrupted. "I have been practicing, baby. You are going to struggle to drink me under the table tonight."

"Maybe I don't want you under the table." I elbowed him playfully.

Dean grinned. "Oh, you are on girl."

Chapter Ten

"I thought you'd been practicing." I ribbed Dean as I threw back another shot. We'd been at Hesitate for an hour. My friends and I had been going shot for shot for most of that time. I was sufficiently wasted. Which is why I chased the shot down with a big drink of water.

Dean shook his head, gave me a smile and threw his back. He chased it down with a beer and sat back on the lounge. "Just pacing myself, baby."

"Time to dance, honey," Sophie sang pulling me to my feet. "This is our song." We'd both changed in the car on the way here. A lot less material in our dresses now.

Laughing as Sophie dragged us to the dance floor, we started grinding our bodies to the beat of the music. By the time Sophie called time out an hour later, I was dripping sweat. We stumbled off to the bathrooms to freshen up, which in my case required splashing a lot of water over my face and neck. This resulted in the removal of all of my makeup, which didn't bother me. Better than being too hot.

Finger combing my damp hair up into a bun, I tucked it in on itself to hold, allowing the cooler air to hit my neck. After the bathroom, we made our way back to the lounges in the reserved seating area. Hesitate was one of Jasper's nightclubs. He'd booked the reserved seating area just for me and my friends tonight, as a birthday present. He wasn't present, which was probably a safety net for both of us.

Alex and Dean sat talking with three men on the lounges. I recognized Warren and Zander immediately, so I knew exactly who the dark-haired man was sitting next to Dean before I saw his face. All the men had lost their jackets and ties. Zander even rolled up the sleeves on his dress shirt to expose the corded muscles in his arms.

Sophie immediately took the only free seat next to the brothers. She grabbed the beer out of Warren's hand and took a big drink. Warren was left staring wide-eyed as his beer disappeared.

"Got a seat right here for you, baby." Dean patted his lap.

Stepping past Alex and Darius, I dropped onto Dean's lap. He picked a shot of vodka off the tray in the middle of the table and handed it to me. Throwing it back, I ignored the unhappy look in Darius's eyes. He only grew angrier when Dean's fingers drew circles on my upper thigh, just under the hem of my dress.

"You look like you are enjoying your birthday." Zander smiled as I picked up another shot. "Did you save me a dance?"

Throwing back the next shot, I stood holding out my hand. Zander let me pull him up off the lounge and followed me down to the dance floor. We started grinding away and were shortly joined by Sophie, making Zander the meat in our sandwich. Alex joined us, pulling Sophie away and starting an impromptu make out session.

Women were moving close, vying to get Zander's attention. One very attractive blond caught his eye. Laughing. I indicated he should go for it. As he turned his attentions to her, I headed back to the reserved area.

"Drink?" Dean walked toward me with two more shots.

"Yes, please." While I threw back another shot, Dean drank his.

When I stumbled Dean caught me, placing me against the wall to stabilize me.

"Time to cut you off, baby."

"Possibly."

"You know these guys?" Dean nodded toward Darius and Warren talking on the lounge, pretending not to watch Dean and me.

"Yeah. I live with them actually."

Dean caressed his finger down my cheek. "So—I wouldn't be in too much trouble if I took off?" He held up his phone. "I got a booty call that I will only say no to for you, baby."

I chuckled. "Go get your rocks off, honey. I'll see you at the altar in the morning."

Grinning, Dean kissed me. Yet again, very chaste. He winked and grabbed his jacket, saying farewell to the others on his way out. With a deep exhalation, I made my way to the lounges and sunk down next to Darius.

"Your score just left without you." Warren laughed.

I shook my head. "Dean and I are not sexually compatible. We flirt, that's it."

"How are you not compatible?" Darius queried sitting back, seemingly a lot more relaxed now.

Picking up another shot, I drank it, hissing at the burn. I probably needed to stop soon.

"I like alpha males," I stated firmly.

"You like to be dominated," Warren clarified, sitting forward, suddenly engrossed in the conversation.

"Yes."

"And he is not alpha enough for you?" Warren raised a brow.

To most outsiders Dean came across as confident and cocky, and he was. In every way in his life he was the one in control. Except in the bedroom.

"Let's just say, that the reason we aren't compatible, is because we fight over who gets tied to the bed." I simpered and picked up another drink.

Warren's eyes widened, then he laughed. "You like dominant men, he likes dominant women. I get it." Warren watched me carefully. "But he still really likes you."

I shrugged. "We are good friends. He swears we will get married some day and make the best husband and wife."

"You don't agree?" Darius asked before taking a sip of his scotch.

I shrugged swallowing the vodka. "I make no presumptions about the future. I would hope, the guy I fall in love with and marry, will enjoy having passionate sex with me regularly."

Sophie's current favorite song came on. A moment later, Sophie was back at the lounges pulling me up to dance with her. "Come on, birthday girl." Sophie laughed stepping up on the coffee table.

I shook my head but went with her. We danced on the table, grinding against each other, not caring that our short dresses grew a lot shorter as we danced with our hands in the air. I bent over to grab two more shots for Sophie and me and nearly fell off the table when she grabbed my hips and spanked me.

Bitting my lip, I closed my eyes, a smile spreading across my face as I stood handing her the shot. We threw our drinks down then kissed each other with open mouths, tongues volleying, hands groping each other.

"Come on! Not this again! Any other girl, Sophie, but not my sister."

Sophie broke away laughing. "She is only half your sister, so you tell me which half and I will kiss the other half."

"Argh, so unfair." Alex pouted, sitting on the lounge.

Warren was watching with interest. "I am not related to either of you. Please feel free to continue."

Sophie laughed again. Winking at Warren, I kissed Sophie again, our bodies still moving to the beat of the music.

"Damn," Warren moaned after a minute.

When I opened my eyes, Warren was rubbing himself through his pants. Kissing down Sophie's neck, I turned her to face toward Alex and nibbled my way up her neck. Sophie took my hand and moved it to her breast, giving me permission to play.

Groping her breast through the fabric of her dress till her nib was hard, I ran a finger across the skin just above her neckline. Slipping my fingers beneath the material, I pinched her hard nipple between my fingers. Sophie moaned for me. She wasn't the only one.

It made me start laughing, killing the moment. Sophie turned her face to mine, gave me another kiss and then stepped forward off the table, going straight to her knees in front of Alex.

I tried to step off the table with the same grace. I failed. In my peripheral vision, I saw Sophie unzip my brother's pants and drop her head. Losing my footing, I fell, right into Darius's lap. Thankfully, not face first, because the solid rod I felt digging into my back told me he'd enjoyed the show too.

"Are you all right?" Darius swept my hair out of my face.

I laughed. "Yes, though, I think it's time to go if Sophie is bobbing for apples with my brother in public."

Darius nodded. "Do you want us to drop you off somewhere?"

I sighed. "I was meant to stay at Sophie's, but it looks like she's going home with Alex." Sitting upright, I slipped off Darius's lap. "I'll get a taxi to my dad's place."

Darius tucked my hair behind my ear. "Come home, Mora. You are intoxicated and I do not want you traipsing across town in this condition."

"I don't want to put you out," I murmured, grabbing my jacket.

Taking my jacket from my grasp, Darius held it for me, allowing me to slip into it. He put his mouth to my ear. "Stop. You asked me not to start a fight with you earlier. Do not start one with me, Mora. I am not put out."

"Are you leaving?" Warren stood.

"The birthday girl is ready for bed," Darius answered.

Warren raised a brow. "Yes, I can see that, but I don't think it is her cold empty bed she is ready for."

Darius glared at Warren. "You think there is another bed she should be in?"

"I can think of at least one." Warren laughed.

Darius shook his head in warning. "Well, her boyfriend is unavailable, so her cold bed it is."

Warren looked where Sophie and Alex were kissing. Walking to them, I kissed the top of their heads. "Night boys and girls. Be safe. Thanks for the presents."

"Well, I might go fishing. Zander seems to have found a nice school," Warren informed.

Darius nodded. "We will see you tomorrow."

"Or Sunday." Warren winked at me before pulling me into a hug.

Darius smirked. "Or Sunday." He held his hand out and I took it.

Clark pulled the car up out front and we slipped into the back seat. We drove quietly. I was watching out the window when Darius placed his hand on my bare thigh and started drawing circles on the inside of my leg. Blinking at him. He was reading something on his phone. Deciding I was drunk and I shouldn't make anything of it, I returned my gaze to the window and enjoyed the sensation.

We rounded a tight corner and Darius's fingers slipped several inches up my inner thigh with the gravitational force. Checking Darius again, he was still focused on his phone screen. Taking a calming breath, I closed my eyes and leaned my head on the window. That's when his fingers found the gusset of my knickers. Keeping my eyes closed, I tried my best not to react.

Finding the side of my knickers, Darius stroked his finger there three times. When I didn't move to stop him, Darius slipped under the material, finding me damp. Inhaling a deep breath, I slid my bottom forward on the seat, spreading my thighs slightly. Taking the invitation, Darius slipped that finger between my folds, stroking that dampness into a trickling creek.

Gripping the seat, I was biting my lip to prevent moaning by the time we arrived at the apartment. Darius removed his hand and put his phone in his pocket. "Thank you, Clark. Enjoy your weekend." Darius smiled as he stepped out of the car.

Sliding across after him, I followed him out. "Good night, Miss Ellis." Clark tipped his hat before he hopped back in the driver's seat and drove off.

Darius was holding the gate for me. He didn't take my hand or try to touch me. Obviously, I'd fallen asleep and dreamed what happened in the car. Inside, Darius took the stairs with me, catching my elbow when I tripped. I started laughing.

"Easy, Mora." He held onto my elbow the rest of the way. Even once in the apartment, he escorted me to my room and inside. "I'm assuming you will be able to change yourself."

Smirking, I lifted my dress over my head. I met Darius's eyes as I dropped the dress to the floor. Holding his heated gaze as I stepped out of my heels, I removed my bra at the same time. Dropping the bra to the floor, I stood there looking at Darius. He didn't move and kept his eyes with mine. Slipping my thumbs under the side of my scanties, I started pushing them down.

"Mora, I do not want you to regret this in the morning," Darius warned as the lace slipped to my knees.

Wiggling my legs, I stepped out of my knickers toward Darius. He didn't back away, didn't make a move to stop me as I reached up and started undoing the buttons on his shirt. Pushing it and his jacket from his shoulders and down his arms.

I felt light, like I was floating. At the same time, I felt hot, feverish, and I knew that feeling Darius's flesh against mine was the cure. Standing there with his heated gaze upon me, my fingers found his belt and the zipper for his pants beyond. Sliding my hands around under the waist of his pants, my fingers slipped beneath the elastic of his boxers, sliding them down.

Kissing down his torso, I squatted to meet his large cock standing at attention. As I came face-to-face with it, large wasn't the word. Monster suited it better. The base was nearly as thick as my wrist, the vein along the base throbbed with his pulse and the smooth head glistened with precum. Licking up the length of him, I sucked that fluid from his tip.

Darius's fingers threaded through my hair. "Mora," he moaned.

I loved the sound of my name coming out of his mouth like that. With no further hesitation, I took him in hand and started licking and sucking the life out of him. There was no chance I could deep throat Darius, I could barely fit him in my mouth, but he didn't complain. He stood there, his moans growing louder, deeper, longer, as I drooled over him, quite literally.

Using my hand to stroke the length of him that couldn't fit in my mouth, my saliva provided lubricant. Massaging his balls, I opened my knees to slide into a bent-knee split, so I was looking at his undercarriage. Stroking his hardness, I licked and sucked his hairless balls. Looking back up at his chest I realized he was absolutely hair free, and it was far too smooth to be from shaving.

Darius was watching me. He tugged my hair to bring my eyes a little higher. "What?"

"You wax."

"I do."

"I think I just came." I hadn't, but my God I was so turned on it was a very real possibility.

Darius grinned large. "Then I better catch up." Taking his cock in hand he aligned it with my lips. "How rough can you take it, Mora?"

Yep, I was going to orgasm without even being touched. "I'll let you know if it's too much."

Offering my mouth, Darius thrust in. He held my head by my hair and moved himself in and out of my mouth with care, pushing toward the back of my throat with each slow shove. Groping his firm ass, I pulled myself onto him deeper. It hurt a little, was definitely uncomfortable, but my God, I loved Darius—in my mouth, that is.

Darius groaned, his rigid member pulsed hard. "Mora?"

I didn't answer. When I flicked my tongue over his head, he lost it. He thrust fast into my mouth and a few grunts later, he was spurting into the back of my throat. My gag reflex kicked in, tears pricked my eyes as my throat and mouth convulsed. I forced myself to swallow. Darius stilled himself, tremors quaking through his body, as I licked him clean before pulling away.

Releasing my hair, Darius stepped back. His breathing was ragged, but he sucked in a deep breath and composed himself. "Get up on the bed, Mora."

Crawling to the bed, not to be sexy, but because I was drunk and didn't really trust standing up without support.

"Stop," Darius ordered when I stood bent over the bed. His hand fell hard on my ass. Jumping a little, I bit my lip. This wasn't the light smack Sophie had given me earlier. Darius had strength behind his swing. When his hand fell again, I swore as the sharp sting and burn radiated through me.

"Darius," I gulped after the third hit.

"Too hard?" he asked, gently rubbing the area he'd just smacked.

"No, but you just finished and I need to be fucked as part of rough play. And I don't mean sex, I mean..."

"I'll take care of you, Mora. You are going to sleep like a baby tonight."

Dropping to his knees before I could say more, Darius gave my dripping sex a long hard lick, his stubble grazing my tender skin. I whimpered. I was so keyed up, I knew that a few more of those and I'd be a puddle.

My fingers kneaded the bed like a cat as he licked, sucked, and bit my heat. My legs started to shake as my body rose quickly to the edge of orgasm. As I breathed his name, he pulled away.

"Lie down." Collapsing on the bed, I rolled onto my back to look up at him. He knelt looking me over. "Do you have any idea how beautiful you are?"

"Says the Adonis in the room." His cock was still erect, nowhere near as large, but I could still use it. Taking it in hand, I started massaging it. "I'm merely a shadow in your presence."

Darius's eyes rolled back in his head. He fell forward, catching himself above me. Darius dropped his head to my breasts and started assailing them. Flicking, sucking and biting my nipples while his hands roamed my body. My back arched under the onslaught and I tangled my fingers into the thick mop of dark hair on his head, electricity sparking through my being.

It was like he knew every pressure point on my body. His fingers would move, find a spot and massage or just apply pressure. I felt utterly out of control. It scared me, and that feeling of safety I normally felt around Darius was washed away with fear.

Darius pulled back, studying my face. "What just happened?"

Sitting up, I wrapped my robe around me. "I don't know. I was really into it, then you were doing that thing with your fingers, and I suddenly felt unsafe and out of control. It scared me."

Darius took my face in his hands. "I would never hurt you, Mora." I looked away. "Mora, look at me," he demanded. "I will never hurt you."

Meeting his eyes, sudden emotions bubbled out of me. Tears started running unbidden. I wiped my tears, exasperated. "What is going on? I feel like I've suddenly got severe PMS. I'm not usually like this."

Darius looked to be thinking hard. "Lay down."

I did, hiding my face with my hands. Darius tapping his fingers over my body lightly, retracing the path he'd been massaging me with, when his finger hit a particular spot. "No," I caught his hand. "That's not where you pressed." Shifting his hand to where he had touched me last. "This is where your hand was."

Darius frowned. "Crap. Are you due for your period?"

I looked at him wide-eyed. "I'm not discussing my cycle with you."

Darius rolled his eyes, "You were just sucking my..."

"That doesn't mean I'm discussing my physiology with you."

Darius lay down beside me and started rubbing his hand across my lower abdomen. "I was using meridian massage techniques to sober you up. I've hit the wrong meridian. If you are due to menstruate, it is very possible you are about to experience your worst ever case of PMS."

"If I'm not due?" I asked quietly.

Darius sighed, caressing my face tenderly. "Then I have inadvertently unblocked a channel that has probably been blocked for a very long time. The emotions you are experiencing are the energy that was locked there."

Yet again, the inexplicable need to cry surged through me. I took a deep breath and tried to push it down.

"You should let it out, Mora. Your body needs to release it," Darius encouraged softly.

Sucking in another breath, I nodded and stood up. Tying my robe around me, I walked to my cello and set myself up.

"What are you doing?" Darius sat up.

Letting the tears fall, I met his eyes. "Letting it out. This is the only way I can do it."

Putting my bow to the strings, I started playing. It was a slow mournful song. I pushed my emotions out through my fingers and into the cello. The tears kept falling as I played, but it wasn't anywhere near as much of a torrent as it could have been.

"That was beautiful. What is it called?" Darius asked as I finished the song.

"Hymn for the Missing."

Collecting his boxers from the floor, Darius came to me. "Come to bed, Mora." He held out his hand.

Setting my cello aside, I put my hand in his. Safety radiated through me from my hand to my shoulder. I breathed a sigh of relief when the feelings Darius usually evoked in me returned. He took me to my bed, lay us both down, and cuddled me into his side, setting us up the way I had last time we'd slept together.

His heartbeat calmed me. After a few minutes, I was more myself again and I could brave talking. "Why did you sober me up?"

Darius kissed my forehead. "I like you sober. You pretend when you're drunk."

I frowned. "Pretend what?"

"That it does not hurt." Darius yawned and snuggled me in tighter.

"What doesn't hurt?" I ran my fingers over his chest.

"Life," he whispered. "It is there in your eyes all the time, in the way you approach everything. When you drink, you try to pretend that it never happened. You lose who you are, and I like who you are, Mora."

"What happened to you, Darius?" I asked drawing invisible patterns over his skin.

Darius sighed. "Sleep, Mora. One day we will exchange our pasts. Not today."

Chapter Eleven

My fingers moved over the finger board as I practiced my scales. The front gate buzzer went off, but I didn't bother getting up to answer. Steffen was there before I would have been able to stand. I continued with my scales, warming myself up. Playing by myself was one thing, helping an orchestral member practice meant getting it right.

"Miss Ellis, your guest is here," Steffen announced as he stepped into the room, Sophie following him in wearing knee high boots and a winter jacket.

"Sorry I'm late," Sophie apologized, walking into the reception room. "Thank you for practicing with me. It is my first time as second chair and I want to be perfect for the concert tomorrow."

Sophie's usual pre-gig jitters made me smile. Tomorrow was the fifth of November. Guy Fawkes Day. Sophie was in the symphony for the main fireworks display in the evening. The last three days had been flat out for Lynwood too.

After the organization of the Halloween masked ball my father threw, everyone was rushing to get things finalized for tomorrow night. Thankfully, Darius wasn't overseeing this one personally, so he'd been a bit more relaxed.

I wish I could say the same. It'd been four days since I'd gone to sleep beside him and woken alone, again. When I'd seen him on Saturday morning he acted as if nothing happened the night before. I wasn't sure if I was relieved or upset about it. I'd taken a deep breath, buried those thoughts, and got on with my job. Did I look at my boss a little differently after blowing him the night of my birthday? Yes, definitely. Did he notice? Probably not.

Sophie thumped her violin down on the dining room table, bringing me back to the room and causing Steffen to wince. Unbuttoning her winter jacket, Sophie shrugged out of it revealing a short, low-cut, long-sleeved dress. Her figure filled it out and then some.

"Could I get you a drink, Miss Trent?" Steffen asked politely, stepping forward to take her coat.

"Only water please." Sophie smiled handing the coat over. Without another thought for the butler, Sophie unclipped her violin case and took out her Stentor. This was her practice violin. She had two performance violins, one a Stradivarius, the other Höfner. All three individually were worth more than her car.

Sophie handed me some sheet music before moving to the piano. Poising her violin, she hit the A key on the piano to tune her violin. It didn't take long to tune, and then Sophie sat in the chair I'd already positioned next to me for her.

"Let's start with Rimsky-Korsakov's Fantasia Number two, Opus. 33: Allegro." Sophie placed her own sheet music on the makeshift stand I'd set up for her.

"Whatever makes you happy." Smiling, I found the sheet music she referred to and set myself up.

We played without talking for the next hour. When we finished the last set, Sophie set her violin across her lap and exhaled.

"You've got this, Soph." I patted her shoulder.

Sophie rolled her eyes. "You always say that. If I played like you, I would have my choice of orchestras to play in."

"You have perfect technique, Sophie, that's not something anyone says about me."

"No, but they say your music has heart. When you play a sad tune, people cry; when you play a cheerful tune, people laugh and dance. Your music gets to the bones of people, Mora."

"And yet, it was you who scored the orchestra position and I work as a personal assistant," I reminded her. "You can't play in an orchestra without good technique."

Steffen walked into the room. I had no doubt he'd been listening while cooking dinner. "Could I refresh your drinks, ladies?"

"I would love a hot chocolate please, Steffen."

"I hate you," Sophie whined. "Just a water for me please. Some of us have to go on stage tomorrow."

I shook my head. "Let's have a break and then we can run through again."

Gifting me a smile, Sophie put her violin on the chair. "Sounds good. You can give me a tour of your boss's pad." Sophie frowned. "Where are the men anyway?"

Understanding the dress choice now, I shook my head. "They were working back and would have gone straight to the gym after work. They'll be back in an hour or so."

"If you are his personal assistant, shouldn't you also be working back?"

"I've done my fair share of late nights the last few months. I told Warren I needed to help you. He told me to leave before Darius got back from his meetings. Come on, I'll show you my room."

Shaking her head, Sophie followed me up the stairs. "Does your boss understand that the P.A. is meant to keep the diary and follow him around like a lost puppy, not his E.A."

I groaned opening my door. "I have no idea why he hired me, Soph. That office would run fine without me. It's almost like Warren needs to look for work for me to do. Except for the errand running, I'm basically sitting at my desk checking over plans and documents that have already been read by both Warren and Darius. I'm just a third set of eyes."

Sophie was looking around my room. "I was about to suggest you quit, but these are really nice lodgings. Especially compared to your last place."

"Wait till you see the view." Opening the terrace doors, I led the way to the sitting area."

Sophie let out a low whistle. "Okay. Do not quit your job. Just take up knitting or something that you can do while bored at your desk."

I smiled leaning on the railing. "I'd miss this place, but maybe I should be looking for something else."

"Not yet. You need at least six months there to make it worth anything on your resume," Sophie advised. "A year would be better."

"My father suggested I come work for him."

Sophie rolled her eyes. "He has been suggesting that for years."

"I'm considering it now."

Sophie's brows jumped. "Why? You have been determined to be independent all this time."

I blew out a breath. "Well, with my father as my boss, I won't be attracted to him."

Sophie studied me. "Things been awkward since the blow job offer?"

"You could say that."

Nowhere near as awkward as having actually done it, and that he'd returned the favor, and spanked me, and made me cry somehow in the process.

Sophie shook her head. "Rejection sucks."

I quirked a brow. "Have you ever been rejected, Soph?"

Sophie thought about it and tipped her head side to side. "Actually, no, but I suspect it would really suck." Sophie took a deep breath. "Speaking of which, can you talk to Alex for me?"

I stood straight. "About what." Sophie batted her lashes. "No."

"Come on, Mora. You know I will make him happier than that cow he is with now."

Walking to the door leading into the hallway, I led the way inside. "Sophie, you knew he had a girlfriend when you started this affair with him. I told you then I wanted to be kept out of it. He's my brother, I can't take sides in this." I led the way back downstairs.

"I'm not asking you to choose between him and me. I'm asking you to choose between her and me."

When I turned to face Sophie, I saw Darius standing in the foyer with the brothers and Steffen, all of them listening to our heated discussion.

"That is picking a side, Soph. I tell him to get rid of Leila and choose you, I've chosen your side. If things go bad between you after that, he will say it was my fault, that I interfered and caused his unhappiness. Alex needs to choose his way forward with the women in his life himself."

Sophie huffed. "You cannot even stand Leila. She is a bitch to you."

"And Alex is well aware of my feelings on his girlfriend."

Sophie grabbed my hand. "Please, Mora. I am utterly in love with him. I want to be more than a regular booty call. He listens to you. You can make him see sense."

I touched her cheek. "Soph, I warned you before this started. I told you not to give him your heart, that you would lose it if you did."

Sophie flinched. "Are you telling me he does not care about me?"

"No. I know Alex cares about you, Soph, but do not mistake that emotion for love." I tried to phrase it carefully. I failed miserably.

"Just because you are incapable of loving someone, Mora, doesn't mean your brother is the same." Sophie stalked over to the music corner, snatching up her violin and sheet music.

"I can love, Soph. I love you."

Sophie snarled. "If you loved me you would convince Alex to leave that bitch and marry me."

"That is emotional blackmail, Soph. It's unfair and I won't tell Alex how to live his life."

"Oh my God, you two are so alike." Sophie slammed her violin case shut and hefted it. The look she got in her eye told me I was about to hear something I didn't want to.

"Do you know he hates that you took this job? He does not want you living here and he really does not like that you have hidden this from your father. Just like you, he refuses to tell you that." Sophie stepped forward to snarl in my face. "Alex thinks your gorgeous boss is going to destroy you, both professionally and romantically. He did not want me to say anything to you, but after last Thursday, I decided it was best you know his fears for you, because *I* care.”

She’d pitched her voice loud enough for our audience to hear. Imagining that hard look entering Darius’s eyes, I swallowed. “You should go now. Good luck tomorrow night.”

Sophie stepped back as if I slapped her. “That’s it? That is all you are going to say?”

Tapping my finger on the back of the dining room chair, I chose my words carefully. “You want to know how I play like I do, Soph? It’s because I take my emotions and convert the energy into my music. You think I’m cold-hearted because I don’t lose my temper and express myself verbally. It’s because I put it all in my music. In that way, you and I are opposite. You are so expressive of your emotions verbally, but stilted in your playing. If you took half of what you are feeling right now and put it into your music, you could be a world class violinist.”

Sophie looked ready to kill me. “You think I am a bad violinist?”

“Take it out. Play what you are feeling.”

“No!” Sophie yelled. “I am angry and hurt. I do not want to stand here playing my violin. I want you to talk to your brother for me.”

Restraining my temper, I stepped past Sophie and went to my cello. Picking up the bow, I started playing. I ignored her, ignored the four men standing awkwardly in the foyer. Closing my eyes, I started playing the frustration that this fight caused me. As I played, I honed in on what was hurting me. Alex told Sophie he thought Darius was bad for me.

Faintly aware of a violin joining with the music I played, I expressed my annoyance in the angst of my music. The breaking heart of the violin broke through the cello’s frustration. Opening my eyes, I watched Sophie. She was losing herself to her music, finally. With a smile, I closed my eyes and continued.

Instead of hurt, sadness played this song for me now. Sadness for Sophie losing her innocence. She was about to suffer her first heartbreak, but from it, I knew she would discover just how brilliant a violinist she was. There was a great future awaiting her after this.

The song drew to an end and I opened my eyes. Sophie was crying. Placing my cello aside, I stepped toward her, uncertain. Sophie set her violin down and threw her arms around me as she started to cry fully. "I am going to lose him, aren't I?" She sobbed on my shoulder.

Unsure how to answer that, I patted her back. The truth was, she'd lost Alex the moment she was willing to be the other woman. Men and women thought about these things so differently. Sophie sacrificed so much to be with the guy she fell in love with. Alex decided if she was willing to be the other woman, then she wasn't good enough for him. I hated that he had that mentality, but it taught me a lot.

Sophie stepped out of my embrace wiping her nose on her sleeve. "I am sorry, Mora." Packing away her violin, Sophie made her way out to the foyer to leave. The men had evacuated the area, possibly taking refuge in the kitchen. I crossed my arms, imagining holding myself together while I waited for Steffen to hand Sophie her jacket and show her out to the elevator.

When the door shut, I took a stabilizing breath. Darius stepped into the reception room, eyes hard, arms crossed across his chest. I shook my head letting him know it wasn't time to discuss this. He gave a small nod, and left the room again. Turning, I grabbed my cello and music stand and walked up to my bedroom. Placing everything down carefully, I collected my phone and called Alex.

"Mora," he greeted happily.

"You need to decide. Leila, Sophie, or neither. You need to make a choice and stick to it, Alex. It's time to man up and put an end to what has never worked for you."

"Mora, what happened?" Alex asked carefully.

"Sophie just left here in tears because she wanted me to convince you to leave Leila for her."

"Mora..."

"I'm not asking you to do that, Alex. It's your choice. Just like taking this job, and living here, and anything else I decide to do with my boss is mine."

Alex took a deep breath. "She told you."

"She was angry and hurt. She wanted to make me hurt as well."

"I am sorry, Mora," Alex sounded remorseful.

"Yeah, you and everyone else. Just end it, Alex. She's in love with you. Don't torture her if you don't feel the same way." I hung up.

***

I was playing my cello as I usually did before bed. It started as a slow moody song and developed into a fast, heavy piece full of angst and pain. I poured my heart into it, feeling every resonating note like a second pulse within me. When I opened my eyes, I felt calmer, more grounded. A clearing of a throat brought my attention to Darius propped in the corner of my room watching me.

"Time to talk." He explained his presence.

Setting aside the cello, I stood. Darius's eyes drifted down my body and back up. Dressed for bed I only wore a shirt with my knickers. Darius wore a pair of track pants and one of his t-shirts which showed ever muscle despite looking casual.

"I didn't tell Sophie about my birthday. Just about you rejecting my offer last Thursday," I clarified straight off the bat. Moving to my bed, I climbed in. I was tired and still had work the next day.

Joining me on the bed, Darius lay down beside me looking at the ceiling. "Okay. Let's discuss last Friday."

"I haven't told anyone about that."

"Not even your boyfriend?"

"Not for the reasons you think. As I told you, Jasper and I aren't exclusive. I'm not hiding that from him. When I see him next, I'll let him know my birthday got out of hand and I went home with a guy. That's all he needs to know. It won't be an issue." I turned my head to watch Darius. "Unless it is an issue, for you?"

Darius tapped his fingers across his abdomen. Recognizing the tapping's of a pianist, I understood the piano down in the reception room, though I'd never heard him play.

"I don't date. I don't sleep with random women either. For the last four years I've been involved with a group of people, mostly married couples, and that's with who I have sexual interactions."

"Swingers." I nodded, understanding. "Why only married couples?"

"They are all wealthy; the women are happily married. I do not need to worry about a woman attaching herself to me for my money. It makes life less complicated."

"Fair enough." I curled onto my side to face him. "So, no issue. I was drunk and randy, you took what I offered. We can leave it behind and move on, keeping our relationship professional."

Darius turned his face to mine. "What if I wanted more than professional? Could we become friends, Mora?"

"I can't see any harm in that."

Darius's smile reflected my own. "Tell me something about you?"

"What would you like to know?"

Darius thought about it. "You told me once about being in the backseat of a car. Tell me the last time that happened."

I frowned. "You aren't going to like that one." I rolled onto my back again.

Darius tapped my nose. "Humor me."

I sighed. "Fine, but you picked it." Mimicking his posture, I started that tale. "I had a boyfriend through high school. He was a nice boy from what everyone perceived to be a good, though, divorced family. His father was a judge and during my younger years, my mother dated his father." I turned to look at Darius. "By date, I mean all bedroom, not much outside of it."

Darius nodded. I looked back to the roof.

"Anyway, our parents hadn't been involved in years when we developed a friendship at school. We were both kind of antisocial and spent a lot of time in the library. He was sixteen, two years older than me, so it surprised me when he spoke to me for the first time.

"At first, we just hung out in the library, and then at cafes. It got around school we were a couple. So, one day he kissed me. We were pretty inseparable after that. His dad was an asshole and he hated him. Since I felt the same about my mother, we kind of bonded strongly. We made plans to finish school and move in together. All the usual teenage stuff. We'd been together two years when I was ready for things to become physical."

Darius raised an eyebrow at me. "Two years with nothing but kissing?"

"Well, there were blow jobs. He was eighteen by this stage." Clearing my throat, I continued. "So, his dad had just got a brand-new Porsche and Daniel, that was his name, decided the car should be broken in and so should I. So, he picked me up, we drove to the bluff and parked, and started fogging up the windows."

"Obviously you did not go through with it." Darius turned his head to look at me. "What happened?"

The tears welled up, but the dam didn't break. "He was doing the pre-work. My phone pinged at the same time his rang. He saw it was his father and answered the phone, just so he could tell his dad he'd taken his Porsche without permission."

The dam leaked, I swiped the tear away. "My message was from my mother. A picture of her new engagement ring and announcing she was getting married—to Daniel's dad. Daniel was hearing the same thing on the phone. He was told he had to break up with me because I was about to be his sister and that wouldn't be right.

"Daniel was livid. He argued that we'd been together for two years, our relationship trumped theirs, but his dad wouldn't have a bar of it. When he got off the phone, we sat there for an hour letting the shock of what just happened settle in. He drove me home, kissed me goodbye and left. The next morning, I got a call from his friend. After Daniel dropped me off, he drove back up the bluff and drove his dad's Porsche off the cliff."

Darius looked at me. "Did his dad have him charged?"

The dam broke, I took a deep breath to prevent sobbing. "He probably would have, but Daniel was in the car when it went over, so he couldn't."

Darius stared at me like I'd grown two heads. "He killed himself?"

"And our parents married in the births, deaths and marriages office the day after his funeral."

"So, they were really concerned," Darius grumbled.

"You know the real kicker? If he just waited, it never would have happened." I stared at the roof. "She hadn't seen him in years, but two weeks before she saw Daniel and I at the cafe kissing. She only went back to the judge to hurt me. Once Daniel broke it off, her interest would have fizzled again. She only dates men for what she can get out of them, or to reach a purpose."

Darius watched me, studying my profile. "She married him."

"Salt in the wound." I turned to meet his eyes. "She insisted they marry the day after the funeral just to hurt me all the more."

Darius looked flawed. "You truly hate your mother, don't you?"

Sighing, I went back to staring at the roof. "She has given me more than enough reason too. My last defying act as her daughter was to send Daniel's diary to a journalist anonymously. It detailed his father's physical and psychological abuse toward his mother and siblings. The journalist did a huge write up on it, since the judge just found a woman guilty of child abuse because she slapped her child in public."

"Did anything happen from that?" Darius asked.

I shrugged and rolled to face him. "I told you, you wouldn't like it. Your turn. Tell me about how you lost your virginity."

Darius hesitated. "I think it is time I went to bed. We still have work in the morning."

Disappointed with his answer, I didn't bother to hide it. "I just told you something I've not shared with anyone else and you don't trust me to even tell about your first time?" I grumbled, climbing out of bed walking toward the bathroom. "Guess this friendship thing has limitations."

Darius grabbed me around the waist as I passed by him and scooped me off my feet, tossing me back on the bed beside him. One armed. I was impressed. "You will judge me badly," Darius defended.

I glared at him. "You just heard how the night I went to give it up to my high school boyfriend he committed suicide rather than fight for me. I'm pretty sure, unless you raped a woman to have sex the first time, that I'd find it hard to judge you."

Darius stared at me a moment then settled back. "We grew up in opposite situations, Mora. No money, it makes people do things to make their life better."

I swallowed. "You didn't rape someone, did you?"

"No." Darius rolled his eyes. "She was very willing, but it was not love or anything like that."

"So, nothing has changed for you over the last decade." I rolled my eyes.

Darius poked me in the side causing me to flinch. He exhaled. "If I tell you this, it remains our secret. It will be covered by the non-disclosure agreement you signed. I will sue you for everything you have and more if you ever tell another soul."

My throat became dry. "I've changed my mind. I don't want to know. Let's just go with your favorite color."

Darius touched my chin and turned my face to his. "I lost my virginity at a brothel. To the madam actually."

My jaw dropped. I mean Darius was gorgeous. How could he not find a girl to have sex with him for free?

Darius took his hand back and started talking as if he read my thoughts. "I nearly had sex with a girl at school once. When she saw my size, she ran from the room, still naked, declaring I was a demon. I believe she became very religious after the experience."

I tried not to laugh, but with the mental imagery, it bubbled up. Darius rolled his eyes, but I saw the smile spreading across his face. He pulled himself up to sitting, leaning against the bed head, legs outstretched and crossed at the ankles. How could he look so good so effortlessly?

"So, needless to say, I decided to wait and not go through that experience again." Darius informed. "I studied very hard to make something of my life so I did not really have time for girls anyway. I won a scholarship to college, but that limited my ability to work and I still needed to support myself.

"That is when I met Zander. He was on a sports scholarship. He was earning a living as a male escort. He loved it. All the sex he could handle, good money, and since only women with money tend to hire male escorts, he was receiving quite a lot of other benefits. He made it sound exciting and fun."

My face dropped. "So, you tried it?"

"Zander worked for a brothel, but not in the brothel. He took me down to meet the madam. She was very keen to have me on board, but needed to make sure I was able to give women the service they were paying for."

I looked at him, pointedly confused. Darius cleared his throat. "That I had a sizable package."

"Oh. Well, I don't think that was a problem." I smirked.

Darius smiled. "No, but I was shy. When she saw the size, she asked to see me erect. I was embarrassed so she got on her knees and touched it. I was rock hard almost instantly. The smile on that woman's face was the biggest I've ever seen. She wrapped her mouth around my cock and started sucking me off. It was my first blow job. I came very quickly."

Darius blushing made me smile to see him embarrassed.

"After that, she wanted to see my recovery speed. So, she kept sucking. I think I came a second time, but I stayed hard for her. She was pretty impressed. Then she asked if I knew how to control myself so I wouldn't hurt a woman. That is when I admitted I had never had sex. She saw fit to remedy that." Darius smiled. "She spent the next week teaching me how to pleasure a woman. After that, I had a job that paid cash in hand and ensured I learned how to please a woman quickly."

Darius's shining eyes settled on mine. I could tell he was thinking about last Friday night as much as I was. Dropping my gaze to the bed spread, I started fidgeting. "So, I should never ask how many women you've been with. Noted."

Darius pressed his palm to my cheek. "The amount I have been with does not count. There has only ever been one woman who was more than sex to me." The way Darius was looking at me was all heat and lust.

"Darius..." I started to shake my head.

Before I could object, his mouth was on mine, insistent and hard. He rolled to put me beneath him and rubbed the object of conversation against me while his mouth possessed mine. I can't say if I would have stopped anything further happening. I barely had the chance to register what was happening before there was banging on the door. Shoving Darius off me, I backpeddled away from him on the bed just before Warren burst in.

He walked straight to Darius who was kneeling looking at me with the most rejected look. Reacting to that look, tears flooded my eyes. Warren put his hands to Darius ear and whispered something. Darius's head snapped to look at Warren, my presence totally forgotten.

"When?" Darius demanded as he stepped off my bed. His eyes now focused elsewhere and just as hard.

"Two hours ago," Warren answered. "Clark is already on his way to take you to the airport and Steffen is packing your bag."

"Good, get the jet ready to take off," Darius ordered as he walked out of my room without another glance for me.

Finally looking at me, Warren's eyes took in how I was huddled against the bed head, my half-dressed state, and the swell of my lips after the passionate kissing with my boss. Warren's eyes flared a little before they dropped to the floor.

"We'll be gone a few days. I'll need you to be me in the office and keep me up to date with everything while we are gone."

"What's happened?" Recovering, I stood up.

"His mother was just rushed to hospital. She has been fighting cancer and the doctors do not expect her to make the weekend," Warren explained.

My heart stuttered at the pain Darius must be feeling. "I'll keep the office running," I assured. Warren nodded. "Warren? Take care of him. He's going to need to let this pain out somehow."

"Darius is one of the most self-actualized people you will ever meet." Warren's smile faded. "It is not Darius I am worried about in this moment."

There was another knock at my door and Zander walked in. "I have packed your bag. It is in the foyer." Zander ran a hand through his bed head hair, his eyes flicking over me. "Everything okay in here?"

"Yes," Warren answered turning to me. "I will call you in the morning for a run down." He turned back to Zander. "Walk me out."

Zander gave me a kind smile then followed Warren out of my room. Snatching up my lounge pants, I tugged them on before walking down the stairs. Warren and Zander were in the foyer talking, but Darius was in the reception room on his phone.

"I will be there as soon as I can, dad," Darius murmured. "Let her know I am on my way." He hung up the phone and turned around. He saw me and his professional mask fell into place. "I will be gone a week. You will need to be..."

Stepping forward, I took hold of his hand. "I know my job," I cut in. "I'm sorry about your mother." I squeezed his hand in comfort.

Snarling, Darius pulled his hand free aggressively, shocking me. "You would dance on your mother's grave. I doubt you could ever comprehend the pain of losing someone you loved."

Darius walked out to the foyer, leaving me there startled and feeling like I'd just been punched in the gut. Hell, maybe he had. My hand instantly went to my stomach clenching at the sudden pain I felt there.

Gasping for breath, I went back to my room. The men all in the foyer as they finished organizing themselves. Darius looked over their shoulders at me as I turned to close my door. Gritting my teeth, I shut my door on the scene below, and on anything I was starting to feel for him. Yes, I knew he was in pain, but the last thing I needed was to become someone else's whipping boy.

Chapter Twelve

"We will be back tomorrow morning," Warren informed me over the phone. Darius's mother died within twelve hours of his arrival. Today was the funeral. "Darius is keen to get back into it and catch up. Can you organize for a meeting with him and the managers for ten in the morning?"

"Consider it done. I will do up a briefing paper for him and email it through so he can hit the ground running. Anything else?" I queried as I sent the meeting request.

"Organize Clark to pick us up in the morning and make sure there is a clean suit in the wardrobe for Dare. If you could bring one in for me too that would be great." Warren sounded tired.

"I'll get Zander to pull one out of your closet for me and Clark will head straight to the airport after dropping me at work in the morning."

"Clark is dropping you at work?" Warren sounded surprised.

"I've been getting into the office early most days. Since Clark usually picks Mr. Rafal up in the morning, he offered to give me a ride until our boss is back. I'll go back to public transport tomorrow evening."

Warren was silent for a long minute.

"Anything else, Warren?" I asked, keeping my voice even. I'd had nearly a week and a half to put my walls back up in place. They were staying there this time.

"No, that just about covers it." Warren exhaled. "Mora?"

"Warren?"

"You have done a great job. When I get back, I am going to give you more responsibility. I know you have been bored."

"Thank you."

"So, you can stop looking for other jobs. We will not be letting you out of your contract. I told Saint Martin's that when they called yesterday for a reference," Warren informed directly.

That explained the call yesterday afternoon from the recruiter. She explained that I did well at the interview and they loved me, but felt it was important I finish my twelve months at Lynwood first. After my contract was finished, they would love to hire me. Pressing my lips tight on my initial expletive response, I decided silence was my best action right now.

"Mora?" Warren checked if I was still there.

I hung up the phone. Great, they were going to block me from finding a new job. I could circumnavigate that by working for Marshall, but I wasn't that desperate yet. If I couldn't get a different job, then I would just have to move out, create a clear divide between work and personal life.

Writing up the briefing paper for Darius, I went to see each of the managers to check that the details were correct. By the time I got back to my desk it was near home time. Zander was sitting at my desk looking at my computer.

"You should lock this when you are away from it," he lectured as I approached.

"People can't get up here without being approved and let up from reception," I replied, annoyed.

"Yeah, but I can, and the managers can." Zander smirked. "I could have been surfing for porn. Every key stroke is logged you know. I can look up and see what sites you have been visiting, so can Warren and Dare." Zander clicked on the screen. "Say you were using your work computer to look and apply for other jobs, I can see that. Or if you were looking at places to rent..."

Glaring at him, I tapped my foot while waiting to get my seat back. "Fine. I'll lock my computer and look for jobs and places to live on my personal computer from now on. Are you finished? I have work to do. Speaking of which, I need a clean outfit waiting here for Warren when he arrives tomorrow morning."

Zander stood. "Jeez, what has your knickers in a knot this week?"

I dropped into my seat frustrated. "Get lost."

Zander frowned at me. "No really, Mora. You have been moody all week. You are playing your cello at all hours of the night. You are barely talking to anyone unless the job requires it, and Steffen said you are barely eating. What is going on?" Zander placed a caring hand on my shoulder.

"That is exactly why I need my own place. So that when I play the cello in the middle of the night, I don't cop an inquisition about why I'm playing it," I grumbled. "Now, unless you have something work related to discuss, I need to get this report to the boss."

Zander shoved his hands in his pocket. "Talk to me."

"Go away," I enunciated.

"Mora?" Opening up the brief, I started making the edits, ignoring Zander. "Come on, Mora. Talk to me. Is this about what happened the night he left?" Zander tried again.

"I don't know what you are talking about."

"Bullshit! Your lips were puffy, your hair was messed, and your shirt was askew. You two were getting hot and heavy before Warren barged in," Zander bit back.

I pressed send on the email. "Looks like I don't have to tell you anything," I replied sharply.

"You can tell me why you are so angry with him. Did you expect him to take you to his mum's funeral, or to stay and finish what he started?"

Standing up, I glared at Zander. "No. I expected nothing of the sort. Nor did I expect for him to accuse me of being a heartless bitch after I just got through telling him about my first boyfriend." Turning off my computer, I started gathering my stuff to leave.

Zander stood straight. "Did you love Daniel?"

That name hit me like a door to the face. Turning around, I stared at Zander. "He told you?"

Zander met my eyes evenly. "He had me check out the story."

I frowned. "Check out the..." When it clicked anger bloomed in my chest. "He didn't believe me? He thought I would make that shit up?"

"Dare is a very careful man, Mora," Zander said, trying to appease.

"Not fucking careful enough," I retorted, my voice growing louder with rage. "I felt like he'd punched me in the gut that night, Zander. That's how bad he hurt me. I felt physically hurt by his words. I don't need that sort of relationship in my life. I'll do my job, but that's it. There will be no more friendly chats in my bedroom or by the fireplace, or his bed."

Zander's eyebrows rose in surprise.

"I'm drawing a line in the sand. He crosses it again, I walk. Job or no job. I will quit and move out of his place so fast his head will spin." I started marching toward the exit. "Tell him that when you report in next."

Shoving the fire door open, I stormed down the stairs.

***

I ran up the fire stairs and into the entry foyer of the executive office. Dropping my iPad on my desk, I checked my watch as I walked directly into Darius's office. It was only eight in the morning. I'd been in at work for two hours already and collected the plans for the two major upcoming events Darius would want to see. I set the two complete plans down on Darius's desk and booted up his computer.

The office door opening caught my attention. I looked over to see Darius in the doorway. "Welcome back." I straightened. "I have the Christmas Concert and New Year's Eve plans here ready for you." Stepping around his desk, I headed for the door. "Did you eat on the flight?"

"No." Darius walked to his desk looking at the plans and his open email.

"Then I'll get you some breakfast and a cup of tea." Leaving his office, I shut the door after me. First encounter, while painful, was done.

Calling the cafe across the road, I ordered him a white egg and salmon omelette. I put the kettle on to boil then picked up my purse and phone and ran downstairs to get it. Fifteen minutes later, I was walking into Darius's empty office again. Placing the omelette and tea on his desk, I assumed he was in the shower and turned to leave.

"Mora?" Darius's voice came from the wardrobe.

"Yes, Mr. Rafal." I turned back.

Darius walked out, pants on but not zipped, shirt still unbuttoned and tie hanging ready to be tied. I hated him.

"We should talk," Darius stated as he buttoned his shirt.

"Did I forget something?" I looked at his desk ticking off every item I knew he would need or been asked to gather.

"No. About you applying for other jobs, looking for another place, about what is happening between us," Darius grumbled, tucking his shirt in and zipping his pants.

"Warren informed me already you will block me getting another job, so that conversation is done. I think it's for the best if I find my own place..."

"I disagree. I do not want you to move out."

"And there is nothing happening between us. Not anymore," I enunciated the last two words. "I told you from the start, Mr. Rafal, I am not my mother. You want to fool around with one of your staff members, diddle Jenn in reception or Hillary in accounting. I'm not interested in being your good time gal."

"Mora." Darius stepped forward, his arm reaching out as if he meant to restrain me.

I stepped out of reach. "No. I let you in and you used what I gave you to hurt me. We are done. You want to stop me finding work elsewhere, fine, but our relationship will be strictly professional from here on out. You can stick your bullshit friendship up your ass."

Darius blinked at me as I turned to leave.

"My mother just died, Mora," Darius tried to excuse his actions.

Peering over my shoulder at him, I opened the office door. "Didims," I replied, not even masking my sarcasm. Darius's mouth fell open. "I'm sorry, was that not appropriate for the moment. I guess I'm just not the person to turn to for comfort. After all, what would I know about losing someone I love?"

Walking out, grabbing my tablet and phone, I marched toward the stairs. Warren came out of the bathroom as I passed, freshly showered and looking professional. "Mora? Where are you off to?" Warren frowned; my anger was obvious.

I didn't stop. "We are out of tea and low on shortbread. I'll be back in an hour."

It was raining outside. I didn't care. It was a fifteen-minute walk to the store that sold the tea Darius liked. In my heels, in the rain, that wasn't the best decision.

"Mora?" Tabitha's voice called to me across the store. Her basket was piled high with various teas and biscuits. "I thought it was you. Why are you so wet?"

"Oh, I forgot my umbrella." Picking up the tea and shortbread I needed, I walked to the counter.

Tabitha frowned following me. "Getting supplies for work?"

"Yes. You?"

"Same. I can give you a lift back to your office if you like?"

Looking down at my shoes, I sighed. "That would be nice, thank you."

Tabitha smiled, her blond ponytail bouncing with her happiness.

After paying for the tea, I stepped away while Tabitha paid for hers. She turned around, her smile wide and engulfing the lower portion of her face. "Let's go."

Following Tabitha out to her car, I slid into the back seat with her. Tabitha looked at her driver. "Jack, this is Mora. A good friend of Mr. Blake's. We'll drop her at work on the way back to the office. She works at..." Tabitha stopped and turned to me. "Where do you work again?"

I swallowed the lump in my throat. "Lynwood Corporation."

Tabitha stopped and stared. "You work for glorious Darius?"

My eyes widened. "Well, I've never heard him called that."

Tabitha chuckled. "Then you have not seen the package he is carrying around. Your boss has the most glorious cock I have ever laid eyes on."

I frowned. "I didn't know you were involved with him."

"I'm not. We have attended some of the same parties." Tabitha winked at me.

"Are you sleeping with Marshall as well?" I asked placidly.

Tabitha's eyes widened. "Uh, no. Marshall is very set about sleeping with his staff. I would in a heartbeat; he is gorgeous for his age." Tabitha lifted a shoulder and dropped it. "I guess he made that mistake already." Tabitha froze. "Oh my God, not that you were a mistake, just that it was a lesson learned."

"It's okay, Tabitha. I know what you meant."

"Are you sleeping with Darius?" Tabitha asked carefully.

I laughed. "I think I'd have known what you meant by his nickname if that was the case, don't you?" Tabitha smiled at me. "I actually find him quite frustrating and annoying. I'm not happy there and looking for another job."

Tabitha nodded. "Darius can be very rigid. He has this rule book he lives by and nothing can make him break it. I like to look at him, but I think working for him would require a lot of patience and attention to detail."

The car came to a stop. "Thanks, Tabitha." I smiled. The driver opened the door holding an umbrella over my head.

Tabitha took my hand. "Mora, if you really hate your job here, Marshall would give you a job without question."

"That's the problem, Tabitha. I want to earn my job, not just have it given to me because of my genetics."

Tabitha nodded in understanding and I slipped out of the car. The driver escorted me to the door where Zander was talking to the doorman.

"Thank you, Jack."

"You are welcome, miss." The driver nodded and went back to the car.

Zander frowned. "Was that Marshall Blake's driver?"

I hesitated. "Yes. I ran into his personal assistant at the store and she offered me a lift back."

Zander looked me over. "You know Tabitha?"

"Yes, she's a friend of the family. I have to get back upstairs," I explained, stepping back inside.

When I walked back into the office an hour later, Warren was sitting at his desk typing quickly. He didn't say anything to me. I walked into the kitchenette and put my purchases away. At my desk I filled out the petty cash claim form and then walked to Warren's desk, putting it in his in tray.

"That pile of files on the corner are for you." Warren pointed to a stack of files. "We are splitting our workload. You seem to have a good working relationship with A.K. so from now on you will deal with the event planning reports. I will take the logistics and on-the-day teams. Sound fair?"

I nodded, picking up the files and taking them to my desk. Finally, I was getting some real work. All it took was me interviewing for another company.

***

"Mora?" Marshall Blake spoke gently.

I looked up from my screen to find my father standing in front of me. "Dad?" I stood up. "What are you doing here?" I looked at the time and knew Darius would be back from his managers meeting at any minute.

"Tabitha told me where you work."

"So?" And I was back to being a seventeen-year-old brat with attitude again.

"So," Marshall mimicked my attitude. "She told me you were unhappy and looking for other work. Is that true?"

I exhaled. "Yes. Though, I'm hoping it will get better now." I tapped the pile of folders. "When Warren found out I was looking for another job he decided to give me more demanding work. I may not need another job now."

"I see." Marshall took a couple of cards out of his pocket. He handed me one. "This is Linda Buchanan's number. She is the recruiter I use for my business. If you decide this is not where you want to work any longer, call her. Linda is the best. Just tell her I recommended you."

"Dad." I sighed taking the card.

"Barring that I have another offer," Marshall interrupted. "Alex has agreed to join me at Blake Industries in the new year. He will be the deputy director and has asked me if you could be his assistant—since you are so determined not to take a leadership role."

I breathed deep. I loved working with Alex and missed him. It was definitely an option I'd like to consider. "I need to think about it."

Marshall smiled, he knew I wanted that job. "You do that."

"Marshall," Darius's voice came down the hall. "Did we have a meeting?" Darius walked up and shook hands with my father. Warren returned to his desk.

"No, I was here to see your assistant," Marshall smiled. "Alex Hark has signed on to work for me in the new year and has requested Mora as his personal assistant as part of his agreement. I decided to come and speak with Mora and see what my chances are of securing her employment."

The smile on Darius's face vanished. His eyes hardened. "Mora is contracted to me till June next year."

Marshall smiled. "Not a problem, I will pay out her contract and even pay for you to recruit another accomplished young lady." Marshall patted Darius's arm then turned to me. "I look forward to hearing from you, Mora." Marshall smiled and started back down the corridor.

Darius glared at me. I met his glare and sat in my chair, returning to my work. Darius turned to the elevator. "Marshall. I will not give her up easily."

My father laughed. "I am afraid, Darius, you will not have a choice in this one. I have been headhunting Mora for years now. It just took me a bit longer to find her Achilles. She will choose her brother over you."

Darius turned back around and stormed into his office. "Both of you in, now!"

Grabbing up my notepad, I walked in with Warren who was looking slightly surprised. "I am not happy with the planning for the Christmas Concert. Some of the performers are not locked in and we are just over a month away. Mora, I expect performance contracts for every named performer by the end of the week. Keep on A.K. till you get them."

"Yes, Mr. Rafal."

"While you are at it, ensure all the performers for the New Year's Eve celebrations are contracted as well. I want the caterers locked in for the Prime Minister's birthday party by Monday and the seating chart by Friday."

"Yes, Mr. Rafal."

"Warren, tell Simon to get his act together. He is not half as prepared for the Cocktail Bonanza Event as he should be. I want it sorted by the end of the week." Warren nodded. "Good. Warren get on that. Mora, stay, we need to talk."

Warren avoided eye contact as he left. Darius indicated the client chair opposite his desk. I sat calmly. As long as Darius kept this about work, I'd be happy.

"You did a good job while we were gone." Darius unbuttoned his suit jacket and sat opposite me in the second client chair. "I was surprised to find out you were interviewing in my absence." I went to defend my choices but Darius held up his finger. "You have said your piece. Now it is my turn. What will it take to stop you from taking Marshall Blake's offer?"

I opened my mouth in surprise. I'd expected anger, not bribery. "Mr. Rafal," I hesitated.

"I do not want to lose you, Mora. Tell me what you need to make this work."

I swallowed. "Keep things professional between us. Stop blurring the lines and don't ever use my past to belittle me again." I met his eyes. "If you can do that, I'll see out my contract."

Darius looked at me for a long minute. "I should never have said what I said. You were being nice, you did not deserve my anger."

"No, I didn't. However, the damage is done and I don't do second chances. Our relationship will be professional or not at all," I stated clearly.

Darius sat forward. "That is really all you want? A professional relationship? No pay rise, special provisions, special treatment?"

Shaking my head, I stood up. "What did I ever do to give you such a low opinion of me?" I walked out.

Warren looked at me when I came out. "Everything sorted?"

"I'm going to speak to A.K. and get on top of this stuff. I might be a while."

Warren's phone lit up. He nodded his head as he picked up the line. "Yes, Dare? You want me to call Zander up? Done."

Grabbing my tablet, I started toward the stairs while Warren called his brother. "Zander. Dare needs to see us. No, it has gotten worse. I think he is going to have to write the whole project off."

Chapter Thirteen

"I need to fly to Munich this weekend for the International Sports Event Management Conference. With Christmas fast approaching, I need one of you on deck to make sure everything is ready for the concert and the New Year's Eve celebrations," Darius directed in our morning meeting.

"I'll stay behind," I volunteered. "Sport isn't really my thing anyway."

"While that is very kind of you, Mora, the Christmas concert and New Year's Eve celebrations have both been handed over to logistics and event management. They are no longer on your roster. Warren will stay behind and you will accompany me to Munich." Darius didn't bother waiting for a response. "We leave Friday night straight from work."

Focusing his attention on his computer screen, Darius ended the meeting. I sighed, standing up. "Do I need to go buy a sports jersey for this conference or something?" Darius smirked but didn't respond.

"You could wear your leotard. I am sure that will definitely bring the vendors over to chat." Warren chuckled, giving me a nudge with his shoulder playfully.

The last month had flown by. Darius stuck to professional interactions and our working relationship was the best it had ever been. I finally settled back into being comfortable at home with the brothers over the last two weeks. With Christmas only a week and a half away, I was looking forward to the break from work and time out from everyone.

I just sat down at my desk when my phone rang. "Mr. Rafal's ten o'clock is here. Mrs. Genhart from Genhart Cosmetics."

"Thanks, Jenn. Send her up." Hanging up, I dialed Darius.

"Yes?"

"Mrs. Genhart from Genhart Cosmetics is here to meet with you."

"That is the launch campaign for a new fragrance, right?"

"Yes, Mr. Rafal."

"Okay, buzz me when she is here."

Logging back into my computer, I looked up information on this conference I would be attending. I was bored after the first paragraph. High heels clacking up the tiled foyer caught my attention. I pressed the buzzer for Darius, he liked to come out and greet his high-profile clients personally. Standing ready to greet Mrs. Genhart, I froze when I saw my mother.

"Mora?" My mother looked shocked. Darius opened his office door in time to hear the rest. "I didn't know you worked here."

"That would probably require you talking to me, *Mum.*" I deserved a high five for keeping my voice even. Darius and Warren were looking wide-eyed between my mother and me. "You've changed your name, again?"

"Yes. I married Bruce Genhart two months ago. I'm the CEO of his cosmetics company now," Eliza informed in her typical obnoxious voice.

"Congratulations. When did you divorce Judge Grady?" I asked, suddenly interested.

Eliza frowned. "Not long after he stepped down for all that controversy over Daniel's diary. Poor Harold lost his son and his job."

"And the wife who caused the first two," I added quickly. "Then again, for a man willing to step over a broken child and leave her there to die, you could probably call it karma."

Eliza forced a smile and turned to Darius. "You must be, Mr. Rafal. It is a pleasure to meet you. Do you mind if we get started? The flight over was quite long and I have a lot to get done today."

"You probably should upgrade your broom to a faster model," I spat.

Eliza snapped her head toward me and glared. "Six years hasn't improved your attitude, Mora." She turned her beaming smile back to Darius. "I don't know how you put up with her, Mr. Rafal?" My mother's eyes skimmed over Darius appreciatively. "Although, you probably have a very adept way of keeping her quiet."

Darius's eyes hardened at the insinuation. Eliza saw it and humbled herself. "I apologize, that was unprofessional."

"Yes, it was." Darius held his office door open.

Eliza turned to give me one last hateful look. "Do be careful on the stairs, Mora." She walked into Darius's office.

Darius spared me a look filled with sympathy. Then he followed my mother, closing the door.

Sitting down at my desk, I took a deep breath. Warren came straight to me. "Are you okay?"

"Yeah, I just need to make a phone call. Do you mind doing the tea and biscuits? I know it's my job, but the opportunity to spill hot tea on my mother is too tempting to pass up." Picking up the phone, I dialed my father's private mobile.

Warren squeezed my shoulder and went into the kitchen to make tea.

"Marshall Blake's phone," Tabitha answered.

"It's Mora. Is Dad available? It's kind of urgent," I asked, deliberately not using Tabitha's name while Warren was in earshot.

"Give me a minute, Mora."

By the sounds over the line, Tabitha walked into a room with what sounded like a presentation taking place. A moment later I heard Marshall's voice. "Excuse me, gentlemen, I have an urgent phone call." There was the sound of movement and a door closing. "Mora, what is wrong?" Marshall asked concerned.

"Eliza is here."

"In London?"

"Yes, but here. She's meeting with Mr. Rafal as we speak," I clarified. "I didn't realize it was her because she's remarried and I didn't recognize the surname."

"I will call John straight away, but I need you to leave now. Catch a taxi to my office. I will have something worked out by the time you get there." His voice was hard and angry. "That bitch will regret ever coming back to London."

"Okay. I'm on my way." Hanging up, I stood up locking my computer. I turned to collect my jacket and bag and saw Warren watching me. "I'm sorry, Warren. I have to go."

"How long will you be?" Warren stepped forward with the hospitality tray.

I grimaced. "Probably the rest of the day. I'm sorry. I know I have that report to do. I'll try and get it done between meetings."

Warren frowned, he'd heard my side of the conversation. "Meetings with who?"

"I'm sorry, Warren, I can't tell you that. Just know it is nothing to do with work." I turned and left before Warren could ask any more questions.

***

Arriving at Marshall's skyscraper office building fifteen minutes later, I was met by Tabitha who escorted me to the elevator. Taking a deep breath, I stepped inside, closing my eyes and imagining a wide open field the entire elevator ride. When the doors opened, I stepped out and held onto the wall as I took very deep breaths.

"Are you all right, Mora?" Tabitha asked, putting a hand on my back.

Assuring her I was fine, I followed her to my father's office. Tabitha walked straight in, holding the door for me, and closing it after I entered. John Hicks sat there along with another man I'd never met before. Marshall stood and walked to me, wrapping me in a big hug.

"Are you all right? That must have been quite the shock seeing her like that." Marshall soothed, rubbing my back. I hated my mother even more. Seventeen years with no parental affection because she was so spiteful, she wouldn't let Marshall have custody or even know me.

Marshall stepped back. "This is Detective Foster. He's going to take your statement and issue an arrest warrant for Eliza."

I frowned. "An arrest warrant?" I thought we were just trying to get the money from my grandmother's house.

Detective Forester stepped forward. "Yes, Miss Blake." The detective used my legal name. "Because you are a British citizen. Despite the fact that your mother nearly killed you on foreign soil, she still attempted to murder one of ours. Therefore, she will be arrested here, and the man who witnessed the crime will be extradited to stand witness and possibly also face charges."

I looked at everyone confused. "But, that was seventeen years ago?"

"It has been twenty-three years since your mother stepped foot on British soil." Detective Forester advised me. "Now, we need to get your statement, Miss Blake."

Detective Forester put his hand in the middle of my back and encouraged me to take a seat. A little stunned. I wasn't expecting this.

"We will wait outside," Marshall informed me as he and Tabitha stepped out of the office.

I felt six years old again, sitting in that hospital while the doctors asked what happened. I'd told them the truth back then. My mother told the police I was a deceitful child and was obviously just trying to get her in trouble. With Judge Grady standing beside my mother, the police did nothing.

John Hicks sat beside me and held my hand when I started to cry. I told my story to the detective. When he asked about any incidents preceding or following that event, I told him how I ended up claustrophobic. Detective Foster's hand shook above the notepad he wrote on.

"You were four?"

"Yes." I sobbed.

"After the stairs, there was no further abuse?"

"My Nan, Freida, wouldn't leave me alone with Eliza after that. Eliza just ignored my existence from there on in," I explained.

"Thank you, Miss Blake. I will need you to come down to the station this afternoon and sign your statement." Detective Foster stood and left.

Marshall came back into the room after he left. "Well?" he spoke to John.

"They have more than enough to put Eliza Ellis in jail for a few years," John answered, rubbing my back.

I sat up. "Jail? I don't want her in jail. I... That just seems so harsh."

Marshall sat beside me. "She will not see the inside of a prison, Mora. Other than the holding cell after her arrest that is."

John took his hand back. "Your mother can afford a very good lawyer. They will plead this down to abuse and abandonment. She will be heavily fined, deported, and never allowed entry to England again."

John stood. "I know you've walked out of an important meeting this morning, Marshall. How about we get lunch and then I will take Mora down the police station to sign her statement and drop her home."

I looked at Marshall. "I'm sorry. I didn't mean to interrupt your day."

Marshall shook his head and wrapped his arm around my shoulders. "Seventeen years ago, I didn't even know you existed. The day I found out I almost lost you. I spent four years fighting your mother for you and she cheated the system. She stole from both of us, Mora. It is time to make her face the consequences of her heartlessness."

"God, I must have broken a mirror earlier this year without realizing it. Life has been like a roller coaster the last six months. So many changes, so many tears. I think I've cried more tears these past few months than I have since I gave up trying to win Eliza's love and approval."

Marshall's arm grew tighter around me. "Alex told me that Jasper and you went your separate ways. That his break up with Sophie Trent has also damaged your friendship. I am sorry it has been a trying year for you, Mora, but I know next year will change all that."

I wiped the tears from my eyes. "I have a report I need to finish for Mr. Rafal before he goes home tonight."

Marshall released me. "Do you always call him that?"

I shrugged. "Occasionally, I call him an asshole, but I save that for special occasions."

Marshall smiled. "How did you end up working for him?"

"Alex's partner Stuart tendered for his business. We met at the meeting. The next day he contacted me and asked me to work for him. As much as I loved working for Alex, I felt it was time I made my own way."

"And it is purely professional between you two?"

I looked at Marshall. "I'm not Eliza."

"I was not suggesting you were. I am merely aware of the effect Darius has on women. You are a beautiful young woman working in close confines with him," Marshall placated.

I patted his leg, "Well, he knows my stance on interoffice relationships, so you don't need to worry, dad." I stood up collecting my bag. "Is there a place I could sit to do my work?"

"Use my desk. I need to get back to that meeting." Marshall stood, kissing my forehead. "Will I see you this weekend?"

"I'm flying to Germany for work. Mr. Rafal needs to attend a conference and, since Warren is flat chat ensuring the last big projects for the year run smoothly, I drew the short straw of accompanying him," I advised. "We'll be gone till Monday. Next weekend?"

"I will be in Paris the weekend before Christmas, but I will fly back Christmas Eve and look forward to seeing you for lunch on Christmas Day."

"Could I stay Christmas Eve and be there for breakfast with you?" I asked quietly.

Marshall smiled. "I would like that very much." He kissed my head again and left.

***

"Are you going to be all right, Mora?" John Hicks asked as his car pulled up outside Darius's apartment.

Eliza Genhart was arrested an hour ago for attempted murder. I'd still been at the station when they brought her in. I'd never seen my mother look so pale and scared. Then her eyes found mine.

In that moment, the regret of not making sure she'd killed me was very clear. The fact that she screeched it across the room made it clear to everyone. If the detective thought for even a moment, I'd been making it up, Eliza ensured that doubt was quickly removed.

I'd been shaken to my core by my mother's hate of me. Literally shaken. I'd spent my childhood striving to be good enough for her love and attention. I think even as a teenager I'd still hoped for one hug, one whisper of praise or love. Just something small to let me know she actually cared.

The words she'd yelled at the police station wiped away any lingering hope that my mother at one time ever loved me. I wondered if even for a glancing moment at my birth, she had looked at the life she created, and cared.

"Do you want to go to the arraignment?" John asked, carefully.

Her arraignment was tomorrow morning. I shook my head. Seeing my mother's hatred for me was enough this evening.

John patted my hand. "I doubt she will be refused bail. She is an upstanding citizen in Australia."

"So are most pedophiles."

John swallowed. "I would feel sorry for anyone stupid enough to piss your father off, Mora. He is a moral man, and he has waited decades to get revenge on your mother for cutting him out of your life. When he found out she was the reason you nearly died..." John shook his head. "He is going to destroy her now. Before, he just wanted you. Now, he will ruin her. It has been seventeen years. He has even more connections. He can make it happen."

Staring at my lap, I was still trembling from the shock of my mother's words an hour ago. I couldn't even really remember what she said. It was like the memory was trapped in a soundproof bubble and all I could see was the absolute loathing in her green eyes. The way she had lunged to attack me, as if she meant to claw my eyes out.

"I tell you this, because if there is even a little part of you that will regret what is about to befall your mother, you need to speak up now and let Marshall know." John gave my trembling hand a squeeze.

As I stepped out of the car, his words floated around the bubble of my mother's hatred, echoing into the shocked cold emptiness of my mind.

Upstairs, I walked into the reception room and found Darius sitting on the lounge reading. Seeing him made my heart beat a little faster. The way he looked at me was in complete contrast to what was running on replay in that soundproof bubble. The confusion was enough to bring my senses back to life. I frowned looking at the time. "Shouldn't you be at the gym?"

Darius marked his page and stood. "I wanted to be here when you came home. Are you okay, Mora?"

"Did you get the report?"

"I did, thank you," Darius replied casually, his eyes watching me like a hawk. Every gesture, every fidget would be analyzed.

"Can you let Steffen know I won't be needing dinner tonight? I'm just going to have a long bath and get an early night." I started toward my room.

"I heard your mother was arrested, and what she yelled across the room at you." Darius gave me that sympathetic look.

"How?" I asked, totally surprised he could know that already.

"Zander has a friend who works at the police station you were at," Darius replied. He looked at his feet. They were bare. He stood there in his suit pants and button-down, the top button undone showing that hollow at the bottom of his throat.

I pictured myself licking that hollow and blinked wide-eyed at the sudden temptation. "I need to go to bed. Today has been rather emotional," I told him quickly, realizing how my brain planned to overcome my sudden emotional upheaval.

"I wanted to say…" Darius stepped forward as if to stop me leaving, "I thought you were just another rebellious teenager, that your dislike of your mother was being over dramatized. I did not for a minute consider a mother could hate their own child so much she could harm it. I could not comprehend how anyone could hate *you*, Mora. You are a kind soul, it should be impossible for anyone to want to hurt you."

I met Darius's eyes. "It is human nature to hate what we fear most. My mother was angry at my father for putting her aside. She was incapable of loving me, so she hated me instead."

Darius shook his head bewildered. "That is what I mean, Mora. Even now you can find sympathy for the woman, after what she did to you. You understand her and accept it. Have you never wanted to lash out and hurt her?"

"If she had been at home when I heard Daniel had killed himself, I would have strangled the life out of her. I think she knew. I didn't see her again until today." I turned toward my room. "Good night, Mr. Rafal."

"Mora?" Darius called as I walked away. I didn't stop. "You do not need to be alone."

"Yes, I do. I've spent my life alone," I murmured and stepped into my room.

After bathing, I dressed in my pajamas, and took up my cello. I lost track of how long I played for. Pouring my hurt into my music, every note resonating with my despair and sorrow.

My fingers were hurting by the time light spilled into my room and Alex was removing the cello from my hands. He pulled me into his arms and I clung to him. He whispered how sorry he was, how I was loved, and that I would never be alone again.

Over his shoulder, I watched Darius shut my bedroom door as he left.

Alex stayed with me. He asked me to tell him the bad stuff, something we'd never discussed before. I told him it all, the claustrophobia, the stairs, Daniel. I let him feel the scar on the back of my head from where I cracked my skull. We finally discussed the harder parts of our lives.

"I always wondered what caused your claustrophobia." Alex stared at the ceiling. "To lock a four-year-old child in the boot of a car for hours on end. Are you sure your mother was completely sane?"

"Sadly, yes." I snuggled into his side and he kissed the top of my head. "Thank you for coming."

"As much as I do not like the way Darius Rafal looks at you, Mora, it was good of him to ring me when he knew you were hurting."

"Yes, it was."

"That or he just wanted the music to stop. You were playing that poor cello pretty hard."

I smirked. "The way it's going, I'm going to need a new cello by the end of the year."

"That one must be getting pretty old by now."

"Seven years I've had it." I smiled. "Nan bought me a new one when I took four-unit music for the high school certificate. She was glad she did when I applied to Cambridge on the music scholarship."

"I am sorry that Sophie is punishing you for me not loving her," Alex murmured. "She should be here with us now, making you laugh, pouring us shots and encouraging you to get sloshed and marry her brother."

I sighed. "Did you end up talking to her?"

"She did not tell you?" Alex queried surprised.

"No. She stopped talking to me the night I called you. She hasn't returned a single call or email."

Alex hugged me harder. "I met with her that weekend. Explained I was not in love with her, and that while I considered her a friend and hoped we could stay friends, we were never going to be a couple in the way she was hoping."

"How did she take it?" I asked carefully and disappointed. I wanted to be there for Sophie when her heart was broken the first time. Instead, I was being held responsible for that heartbreak.

"She poured a glass of wine over my head and walked out. I think you prepared her for the worst of it."

"So, Leila is the one?"

"God, no." Alex winced. "I broke up with her that weekend too."

I looked at Alex. "That was over a month ago. Why didn't you tell me?"

Alex stroked a finger down my face. "The next weekend I was going to tell you, but there was this intense sadness in your eyes. I hated that I caused you to lose your best friend."

I sunk back on the bed. If only that was the real reason I'd been so miserable a month ago. "I feel like all these doors in my life are slamming shut in my face."

"Then there is a path you are meant to be taking that you are avoiding," Alex offered wisely. I looked at him. He shrugged. "You are fighting the path fate wants you to take. As you try to step in a different direction it is closing that path so that eventually you are not going to have an option but to walk the path preordained for you."

We sat in silence for a moment. "You come up with some shit sometimes, you know that, right?"

Alex chuckled. "Maybe, just maybe, you need to look at what you are resisting. It could be where you are meant to be."

My mind instantly went to Darius, naked as I knelt before him. Nope, that was hormones. Fate would have kept him clothed.

"Maybe," I murmured.

The next morning, I sat in Darius's office while he and Warren discussed a few issues that had cropped up. I don't know at what point I tuned out and started watching the snow outside the window. I know that when a phone rang out in the office, I turned back to the room to find Warren gone and Darius working quietly at his desk.

Glancing around with a frown, I then looked at my watch. Thirty minutes had passed. Standing up, I started to leave.

"Do you need to take some time off, Mora?" Darius asked behind me. When I turned around, he was watching me.

"No. I'll be fine," I responded hollowly.

"Fine." Darius rolled the word in his mouth. "The female equivalent for being the exact opposite of what the word implies. Freaked out, insecure, neurotic, emotional, I believe is the true definition?" Darius stood up. "Yes, I believe you are indeed *fine*."

"I always thought the F stood for fucked up," I answered sadly. "Thank you for calling Alex last night."

Darius dropped his hands into his pockets and blew out a breath. "I love hearing you play, Mora, but last night was torture. Beautiful, but torturous. Because I now know you play your emotions." Darius took another step toward me. "Take the day off, Mora. I do not know where you are, but it is not here at work."

"I was told last night I need to decide how badly I want my mother to hurt. My father has the power now to ruin her, and he will, unless I step in," I confessed.

"You are struggling with the morals of destroying someone so thoroughly and the longing to see her suffer?" Darius nodded as if understanding.

He took another step forward, lowering his voice. "You told me last night we hate what we fear the most. You fear becoming like her. You basically admitted it to me the day I kissed you in the library. I should have realized then, but I understand now, why you were so angry with me. You related what happened between us as a sign you were like the woman you hated. I'm sorry, Mora."

I was struggling to hold my emotions in. "What do I do?" I whispered.

"What would your mother do if the roles were reversed?"

I gave a sad laugh. "She'd destroy me in a heartbeat."

Darius ducked his head to catch my gaze. "Then you have your answer, Mora. Do not be her."

Startled he made it that easy to know the right path, I wanted to kiss him. He was right there, all I needed to do was step into him and I could press my mouth to his.

Darius's eyes flicked between my eyes and mouth. He touched my cheek, and stepping into me, moved my face to his shoulder as he hugged me ridiculously tight.

"Mora, you wear your god damn heart on your sleeve," he murmured to my ear. "It is killing me."

Darius let me go and walked out of his office, leaving the door open, not looking back. On his way to the elevator he called to Warren. "Mora will be taking a personal day."

***

"Did you go to the arraignment?" I asked Marshall while we waited for our meals at his favorite restaurant.

After leaving work I called him and asked to meet for lunch. Marshall made room for me immediately.

"Yes. She was denied bail. They consider her a flight risk and, after the way she lost it at the station last night, the judge decided she may pose a potential threat to your welfare," Marshall informed me. "The courts close for Christmas tomorrow. Your mother is going to spend the festive season behind bars."

I struggled to breathe over a ball of guilt in my throat. "I don't want to destroy her, dad. She is evil and horrible, but she never threw me out on the street, she still provided for me. She never destroyed me."

"Wrong. I provided for you. If she had thrown you out on the street it would have voided the family court orders. She knew I would have been there in a heartbeat to bring you home," Marshall corrected. "She could not destroy you because you were strong, and because Freida protected you. Have you ever thought what your life would have been like if Freida had not been there?"

I had actually. Quite a lot in my early teens. I wondered if I would have survived. I was surprised by what Marshall added to that. I'd never considered once, that the only reason she allowed me to stay under her roof, was to stop Marshall gaining access to me.

Marshall sighed. "She will stay in jail till the new year. She will get time served, be deported and never allowed to return. I will ensure the Australian courts are aware of her corruption of the court system and leave it there. Is that acceptable to you, Mora?"

I nodded, tears rising to the surface, the strong emotions I felt stealing my voice.

Marshall took my hand. "I will never forgive her for not letting me know my own daughter, and for hurting you. I admire that you would show her mercy."

"I want to see her." I whispered the words before I realized I'd even thought them.

Marshall caressed my cheek in a fatherly way. "Let me make a phone call." He slid out of his seat effortlessly. I'd never considered how fit he was for his age. When he came back to the table he looked a lot more relaxed. "After lunch."

Marshall came with me. We drove to where Eliza was being held. Detective Forester met us and escorted us in. "Are you sure you want to do this? She was pretty aggressive to you last night." I nodded. "Is this a closure thing?" I nodded again. Forester exhaled. "It is rare for abusers to regret their actions. You may walk out of here with nothing more than more abuse, Miss Blake."

"I lived with that woman for seventeen years, Detective. I am well aware she will offer no apologies for her treatment of me. I am not here for her regret. I'm here to close the door for good." My confidence was slipping back into place with every step we took.

Forester met my eyes. "Then I wish you luck." He opened a door and stepped back. "Your father and I will wait next door."

Stepping inside, my mother sat handcuffed to the table. Moving to the empty chair, I sat down, her green eyes following my path. The anger in them was burning her alive. I don't think I'd ever seen her without makeup and her hair styled perfectly. She looked so much older.

"Well, you must just be happy as Larry, little girl. You finally got the upper hand on me."

"Shut it," I spoke clearly and met her eyes. Eliza was stunned and sat back as far as the cuffs on the table allowed. "I didn't come here for your bullshit. I came here to let you know prison isn't the goal for me here. I'm not you. I am not going to walk out of here happy for seeing you look a mess and the expectation of seeing your life destroyed."

"Then what are you here for?" Eliza sneered.

"I want you to know that the next time you appear before the judge will be your last night here. You will be deported back to Australia and I will never have to see you again. Yes, you are going to have a criminal record here. Yes, it is probably going to affect your life back in Australia. Frankly, whatever happens to you now is karma. A few weeks in jail isn't going to make you a nicer person. It's important you know, I'm the one showing you mercy here. I'm the one with a heart. Unlike you, I can forgive."

I stood up walking back to the door. "Though," I turned and smiled at my very unhappy mother, "I won't object to them driving you to the airport in the trunk of a car. Just for you to have that experience."

"The amount of times I gave fate the opportunity to snuff you out, and yet you live," Eliza sniped.

"Maybe I was your punishment for being such a conceited fucking bitch." Eliza glared at me. Giving her a small shrug, I walked out.

Detective Forester shut the door and motioned to a guard waiting nearby. Marshall put his arm around my back and walked me out. "I am proud of you," Marshall murmured.

I was shaking, but I wasn't sure if it was fear or relief. After thanking Detective Forester, I walked outside with my father.

"I will give you a lift home." Marshall walked toward his waiting car.

"No, it's okay. I'm going to walk. I need some time to myself."

"Mora, it is snowing." Marshall pointed out the obvious.

Gifting him a sad smile, I kissed his cheek. "I love the snow." I walked off, enjoying the snow on my head, letting the tears run down my cheeks, contradicting the smile on my face.

Chapter Fourteen

When we reached the steps to the private jet I nearly balked. Darius continued on unfazed and was already at the top of the stairs. I didn't even consider we would be flying in a small plane. Not that jets are small, but they are smaller compared to big planes.

Taking a deep breath, I focused on putting one foot in front of the other, and climbed the stairs. Yesterday I'd faced my mother, today I could conquer my claustrophobia.

Darius was already seated with his laptop out in one of the first seats. Moving to the last lot of seats and the other side of the plane, I slipped into the seat closest the window. I unzipped my boots and shoved them under the seat.

"Can I get you anything, miss?" A hostess smiled at me.

"Valium?" I joked.

She gave me a gentle smile. "Scared of planes?"

"No. Enclosed spaces. On the ground, in the air, doesn't really matter."

"Just relax. If it gets too much, we have vodka." She winked.

I considered asking for that vodka now, but Darius had a no drinking while working policy. Not that I had recovered from the last time I drank vodka and was alone with Darius. No, I think alcohol needed to be outlawed while I was anywhere in the vicinity of Darius Rafal.

The plane taxied and took flight. I watched carefully out the window.

"Are you hiding from me back there?" Darius asked as the seatbelt sign switched off.

"No." I didn't take my eyes off the scene out of the window. "How long a flight is it?"

"Two hours," Darius replied. "It will be another hour to the hotel we are staying at."

It was already seven o'clock. "So, ten o'clock before we reach the hotel."

"Germany is an hour ahead of us. It will be eleven when we arrive." Darius watched one of the hostesses approach him with a glass of water. The buttons at the top of her blouse seemed to have come open showing all her cleavage and part of her red lace bra.

"Mr. Rafal," she purred before getting on her knees in front of him.

Darius caught her hand as she reached for his fly. "No, thank you, Tracey."

Surprisingly, Tracey didn't seem offended by the rejection. "Let me know if you change your mind, Mr. Rafal." She got back on her feet and went about her duties. I went back to looking out the window.

"I have never seen that nervous gesture before." Darius sank into the seat beside me.

Stopping, I looked at him, then down to my left hand which was playing my right upper arm like a fingerboard on the cello. With great effort, I dropped my hand back to my lap. "Insecurity."

"You play yourself when you are feeling insecure and your cello is not handy?" I nodded. "Interesting."

"Is it?"

"Very. What on Earth could you have to feel insecure about, Mora Ellis?" Darius's eyes flicked to the hostess with the mostest. "Ah, you saw that. I thought you were still staring out the window."

I turned my gaze back to the window. "Your plane, your game."

"Still, I want you to know, Tracey is only utilized when I am significantly stressed."

I exhaled long and hard. "Mr. Rafal, while I appreciate your honesty, you getting your dick sucked by another woman is not my concern right now. I am claustrophobic, on a small plane, and I cannot drink alcohol because the last time I was drunk near you I was the one sucking your monster of a cock." I slapped my hand over my mouth. "Shit, I'm sorry. That was unprofessional."

"Would you prefer to be sucking my cock now, Mora? It might take your mind off the confined spaces," Darius offered civilly.

God yes!

"No." I sighed, ignoring that devil inside me who unfurled for the first time in weeks. "Shit. I can't be thinking about this right now."

Darius smirked. "Would it help if another woman sucked me off in front of you. Would you be less tempted then?"

"I'm not tempted!" I snapped. "It's just..." *been a very long time.* I took a deep calming breath. Darius didn't know I wasn't seeing Jasper anymore. "...been a very stressful few days," I covered.

"Tracey can take care of you instead if you prefer, Mora? She is bisexual and happy to put her mouth to use wherever it is needed."

"Crossing that line, Mr. Rafal," I warned.

"I disagree, Mora. Tracey has happily serviced clients and friends of mine before. It is her job."

"Wait. You hire her just to suck off you or your clients?" I wasn't disgusted. More intrigued.

"Yes, and she doesn't just suck. She fucks too. She also has qualifications in massage therapy." Darius watched me carefully, his eyes sparkling. I wasn't sure if he was trying to rile me up or being honest.

"Her service sounds well-rounded," I replied evenly.

"Very." Darius stood up. "Tracey?" The busty brunette instantly sashayed toward us. "Mora needs a relaxing massage. Take care of her for me please."

"Of course, Mr. Rafal," Tracey purred. "This way, Miss Ellis."

When I went to protest, Darius gave me a stern look. "I am ordering you to have a massage, Mora. You are stressed. Let Tracey take care of that for you." Without another word Darius walked back to his seat and focused back on his laptop.

With a sigh, I followed Tracey to the massage table bolted to the plane behind my chair. I hadn't recognized what the bench was when I first came on board as I was too focused on not freaking out.

"Remove your clothes please, Miss Ellis." Tracey smiled as she heated some massage oil.

With a look over my shoulder to ensure Darius wasn't watching, I slipped out of my jacket and unzipped my pinafore. Letting it drop to the ground, I slid my stay-up stockings down my legs. Tracey watched with a smile. She indicated my underwear. Swallowing hard, I unhooked my bra before sliding my underwear down my legs.

Tracey patted the table. After I lay down on my stomach, Tracey poured the hot oil on me. I had to admit, by the time she'd finished my back, I was a lot more relaxed. She was very good with her hands. Toweling off the excess oil when she'd finished the back of my body, Tracey stepped back. "Roll over when you are ready please, Miss Ellis."

Once I rolled onto my back, Tracey covered my torso with a warmed towel, my eyes with a scented eye pack. I realized the bench itself was also heated. Damn, I could get used to such luxuries.

Tracey started at my feet and worked her way up. After my hands and arms, she moved behind my head and started massaging my chest. I was just zoning out when her hands slipped under the towel and cupped my breasts. She massaged them, then, pushing the towel lower, she massaged my ribs below my breasts.

A moment later her hands were back on my fun bags.

"You have lovely muscle tone," Tracey commented. "And such lovely firm breasts. Are they natural?"

"Yes."

"Mine aren't." Tracey grinned. "Cost me a year's wage, but worth it."

Tracey continued to massage my rib cage and breasts and I lay back and enjoyed the attention. Biting my lip, I resisted squirming under the attentions of her hands. After several minutes, Tracey pulled the towel back up and moved to my thighs.

"Butterfly your legs for me. I'm going to massage your inner thigh and it's much easier to reach like this," Tracey advised, assisting me to bend my knee out to the side. "Impressive flexibility. Are you a dancer?"

"No."

Tracey's fingers started working up the inside of my inner thigh. She did both legs and then adjusting her position and the towel, her hands scooped across my lower abdomen and started massaging my pubic mound gently. Her hands slid to either side of my labia and she massaged that area where your inner leg joins the torso. I relaxed into her touch, months of tension being drawn out as she worked her fingers.

"You store all your tension in your groin," Tracey murmured. "I was wondering why I couldn't find any in your shoulders. You must use sex as your stress release for all your tension to coil here."

Since I was too busy turning into a puddle of mush under her fingers, I didn't respond. She didn't touch my sex, just massaged all around it. When she massaged above my clitoral hood my body coiled like a viper.

Tracey laughed. "Honey, you have a lot of stress stored here." She chuckled quietly. "Let's get that taken care of."

Her hands disappeared from my body for a moment. The sound of the hot oil bottle being squeezed preceded the warm dribble over my folds. A solitary strong finger followed the trail, separating my labia and inserting itself slowly inside me. Tracey's fingers felt bigger and stronger. Stroking inside me with that one large finger coaxing the pleasure pit inside me to yawn open.

That finger caressed me till I relaxed a little more, then a second finger pushed in. Gripping the side of the table at the sudden full sensation, it took everything in me not to moan out loud. With sight out of commission my other senses heightened. My sense of smell really picked up on the floral notes of Tracey's perfume, the sweet almond of the massage oil, and then men's aftershave.

Inhaling deeply, focusing on Darius's scent, the devil inside me somersaulted at the thought of his fingers being inside of me. With that simple addition, I came. My back bowed and I opened my mouth, suffocating as my body bucked and pulsed.

The eye pillow started to slip but Tracey's free hand covered it to hold it in place. Holding the mask there, she removed her fingers, wiping over my labia before moving the towel to cover me. Finally, she took her hand from the eye pillow and whispered in my ear. "I bet you feel better now."

Better was not the word I would use. I felt wonderful. So relaxed it wasn't funny.

"When you are ready, pop yourself up and redress," Tracey purred, removing the eye pillow.

"Thank you, Tracey." Clasping the towel to the front of me, I sat up slowly, and slightly unsteady. My eyes still adjusting to the light and blood flow returning to my head.

Tracey looked at my eyes. "Wow, you really needed that, didn't you?"

I blushed. "You are very skilled with your hands."

Tracey chuckled. "You should have Dare give you a rub down. That boy offers heaven with his touch."

Her casualness with Darius interested me. She was older than Darius, but not by much. "Have you worked for Mr. Rafal long?" Watching Tracey clean up, I slid off the table and pulled on my underwear so she could wipe down the table.

"Since he became someone. We've been friends since college. We worked together till he finished his degree and then when his company started becoming known, he employed me to take care of Nahum. I manage that, and when he's flying, I fly with him," Tracey divulged quietly.

"Nahum? I've never heard of him."

Tracey looked over at me unsure. "It's not a he. It's a place. Several places actually. Nahum was Dare's first business venture. It gave him the money to start Lynwood." Tracey turned to assess me. Her eyes flicked back to where Darius sat talking on his phone. She lowered her voice. "Look, you probably shouldn't mention that. I thought as his P.A. you would know."

"It's okay. I won't say anything."

She tilted her head looking me over. An intelligence I'd missed earlier shined back. "You're not what I expected. When he first told me about you, I expected a prim and proper little princess."

"Prim and proper have never been used in the sentence describing my personality."

Tracey smiled. "I can see that." With a wink. Tracey sauntered to where Darius sat at his laptop. "You're such a naughty boy," she purred as I strained to hear her. Stealing his hand, she sucked two of his fingers into her mouth. "Hmm, that tastes good."

"Shh," Darius hushed her quietly.

"Your turn now?" Tracey raised an eyebrow. "I can see you need it."

Darius shook his head. "No, thank you, Tracey."

With a shrug, Tracey made her way to the staff area while I turned my attention back to getting dressed. Zipping up my pinafore, I sat down to put my stay-ups back on when Darius appeared next to me. He watched me settle the first stocking into place at the top of my thigh.

"Feel better?"

I swallowed. "Yes. Thank you."

Darius took my other stay-up and readied it. He held it for me to place my foot into and slowly slid it up my leg. His touch sent sparks through my body. The devil inside smiled and started dancing to his tune.

Directly in my line of sight was his groin. His hard-rigid cock that was causing a tent effect in his pants. The desire to release his monster and let him play with my devil was too much. Closing my eyes, I breathed deeply. Gasping as his finger brushed my upper thigh. "Line, Mr. Rafal."

"If you just came you would not still be reacting like this to my touch."

"I don't work like that. With foreplay orgasms, I'm still left wanting."

Darius withdrew his hands. "You are not satisfied until you get plowed?"

Blushing, I slipped off the table. "Again, Mr. Rafal. Line."

"You intrigue me, Mora. Is it so wrong that I try and understand you better?"

I met his eyes. "If that was just the case, no. Right now, however, your monster is trying to escape his confines, which makes this not so much about psychology, but lust. Therefore, line."

"Mr. Rafal, we are starting our descent into Munich. If you could take your seat please?" The actual flight attendant asked.

Slipping into my seat, I belted myself in for landing. Darius moved to his, closing his laptop and packing it away. This was looking to be a very long and frustrating weekend.

***

We arrived at the hotel where the convention was being held just after eleven. Darius went to check us in while I collected our bags from the driver—my standard cabin bag, and Darius had one of those professional suit pack bags with a trolley case. It allowed room to pack important things like toiletries while keeping his suit wrinkle free.

By the time I walked inside, Darius had our room keys. He relieved me of his bag and I followed him to the elevator. Once the elevator doors closed Darius took a deep breath. "Here, look at this." Darius shoved his phone at me.

It was an email confirming two rooms booked in Darius's name requesting side-by-side rooms. "Okay?" I handed the phone back.

"I wanted you to see that before I told you they messed up my reservation," Darius began. The elevator opened and he led the way down a corridor. "They did not book a second room for you." Darius stopped in front of a door and looked at me.

"But they fixed that up, right?" I asked unhappily, having a feeling where this was going.

"The hotel is booked out for the conference, Mora. There is no other room to give you. We will need to share." Darius slid his key into the lock and pushed open the door. He walked immediately into the bedroom and disappeared.

173

Standing in the middle of the living room, I stared at the massive bed, the focal point of what I had to admit was a stunning suite. It was situated at the top of the corner tower, and held a fabulous circular bedroom surrounded by five windows offering one-eighty-degree views of the city's enchanting red roofs and ornate spires. The bedroom contained a king bed that I was going to share with Darius. Yes, I'd shared a bed with him previously, but that was before my birthday.

The rounded sliding doors allowed the bedroom to be closed off from the adjacent living room, which was furnished with a large sofa, three armchairs and a desk fashioned from cherrywood. I considered sleeping on the sofa; it would have to be a safer choice.

"Mora?" Darius called.

With a deep breath, I followed his voice. Turning to the side, I stepped through a door into the elegant marble bathroom. It boasted a separate walk-in shower, deep soaking bath and access through a walk-in wardrobe to the bedroom. Yet again, that giant bed dominated my view. That was, until Darius stepped into the bathroom in just his boxers.

"It is late. Unpack and get into bed. You have not really slept the past two nights."

Walking past me, Darius turned on the taps to the shower. Without a thought to me still being in the room, he dropped his boxers and stepped under the water.

Watching that hot water run over his nude muscular body, I groaned. It was only made worse when I realized his gorgeous monster was growing thick and hard, standing at attention.

Darius wiped the water from his face and met my eyes. I watched as he took his monster in hand and he started stroking himself. Darius watched me watch him, my feet rooted to the spot, unable to look away.

"Mora, go to bed," Darius ordered.

"I'm sort of captivated right this second," I explained meeting his eyes. It's like he held me captive with his gaze.

Darius pumped his cock. "Do you want this, Mora?"

"Yes," I answered honestly before I could help it.

"Then come over here."

"I can't."

"Because of the line?" Darius guessed.

"Because of the line."

Darius sighed. "Then go to bed, Mora, because if you stand there another minute, I am going to pull you into this shower and spend the night doing bad things to you. Things which will cross more than just your professional line."

"Like what?" Okay, I probably shouldn't have asked, but my line didn't count out masturbating thinking of Darius, and I am not going to admit how many times that happened over the last month.

Darius grinned. Releasing his cock, he put a hand on either side of the shower opening, showing himself off beautifully. Damn it, the look in his eye told me that he knew exactly how good he looked standing like that. "Have you ever had a man cum in your ass, Mora?"

My eyes went wide. He had to be kidding. That monster couldn't fit in my mouth. I'd struggle to have him in my clutch. There was no way he was going to fit up the back passage.

"No." Closing my eyes, I exhaled. Pulling strength from deep inside, and trust me, it took a lot of strength, I turned my back on Darius and walked back out to the living room. I was definitely sleeping on the lounge tonight.

Opening my cabin case, I expected to find my pajamas, only, they weren't there. "You have got to be kidding me," I growled in frustration.

I swear I'd packed my night shirt in. In fact, I distinctly remember folding and packing it so it was right on top. Then I took my bag down to the foyer, and left it ready for Clark to collect.

Huffing a breath of frustration, I determined which one of the four men in the house needed to be murdered for repacking my bag. And it was repacked. Looking at it now I could tell that. The new underwear I'd purchased with Warren's gift voucher was packed in, the two skirt suits I'd packed to wear for the weekend were swapped for the more expensive dresses that Darius bought me. Everything was different except my toiletries, and there were no pajamas.

Slamming the lid shut I picked up my phone and dialed Zander.

"Hello, beautiful. How is the trip?" Zander chuckled.

"I'm going to kill you, and Warren, and even Steffen if he was involved," I threatened.

"Calm down, beautiful. We just wanted you to look your best." There was laughter in the background. I recognized Warren's voice when he commented on how much he liked the present he bought me.

"Zander, you forgot my pajamas and I'm sharing his bed," I growled in a low voice.

Zander sobered. "Wait, what?"

"The hotel messed up the reservation and only booked us the one room. You've left me nothing to wear to bed."

"Crap, Mora. We did not mean for that to be the situation." Zander sounded worried.

"What situation were you hoping for?" I asked angrily.

Zander swallowed. "Well, the sort that Warren and I got to go to sleep knowing you were in bed naked."

"I thought you looked at me like a little sister?" I grumbled.

"Dare will not allow us to think of you otherwise," Zander answered remorsefully.

"And yet, I'm down a set of pajamas." I hung up the phone. "Shit."

Taking my bag into the wardrobe, I noted Darius was still in the shower. Yes, I looked, and yes, he was still stroking. Thankfully, he had his back to the wardrobe.

Yanking my boots off, I reached around and grabbed one of the robes from the bathroom before moving back into the bedroom and stripping. Pulling on the robe, I hung my dress up in the wardrobe and went to use the separate powder room to ready for bed.

When I came out, the shower had stopped. Tiptoeing into the bedroom, I observed Darius brushing his teeth in the bathroom. Walking to the bed, I pulled back the quilt, removed my robe, leaving it on the floor beside the bed, and turned off the light as I climbed under the covers. Snuggling down into the comfortable mattress, I stared at the window opposite.

In the reflection, I could see Darius when he stepped into the wardrobe. Walking to the bedroom door, Darius stood there looking over the bed. He ran his hand through his hair and murmured something to himself before switching the bathroom light off, leaving the room in darkness.

I didn't feel Darius climb into the bed, but I heard the quilt as he settled himself. "Mora?" Darius murmured quietly.

I didn't answer him, pretending instead to be asleep.

Darius moved again. "I cannot believe how badly I have messed this up," he whispered forlornly. He was being a bit harsh on himself. He couldn't be blamed for the room mix-up. The bathroom? Yeah, that was totally on him.

"I am torn, Mora. I want you to take the job at Blake Industries just so I am not your boss any longer. However, I would miss you, and you are good at your job. I think Warren would kill me if I fired you." Darius took a deep breath. "I really wish…"

My phone started ringing. Wincing, I wanted to curse whoever was on the other end. Pretending to have been woken up, I grabbed my phone from the nightstand and looked at the caller ID before I answered. "Alex?"

"It's Friday. Where are you?" He yelled over the clamor of a night club behind him.

"I'm in bed. Where are you?" I responded unhappily.

"J.J's. Get your ass out of bed and get down here. Jasper is here and looking for you. You should see the ring he bought, Mora. It is stunning. You are going to die when you see it."

Having no doubt that Darius could hear both sides of the conversation, I cursed. "That's not going to happen, Alex. I'm in Germany."

"You are where?"

Alex disappeared from the line and I could hear yelling. Suddenly the other side got quiet. "Come on, Mora. Get your ass down here," Jasper's smooth voice coerced.

"I'm in bed already, Jasper," I whispered.

"So, get out of it, and why are you whispering?" Jasper laughed.

"Because I'm not alone in the bed, Jasper."

"Oh." Jasper went quiet for a moment. "Shit, baby. Is it the guy from your birthday?"

"Yeah, it's the same guy." Cringing, I hated that Darius could hear this conversation. I would have left the room, but I was naked and hoping Darius wouldn't notice.

"So, he has become a regular thing then?" Jasper asked, curious.

"No. Not at all. This is only the—it doesn't matter. It's not that," I answered clumsily.

"Are you sure, baby? You do not sound sure."

"I'm sure. He's a work colleague."

"What the? Are you trying to lose your job? Didn't Rafal say no work romances?" Jasper sounded concerned.

"Yes, Mr. Rafal did put an edict out against me being involved with *anyone* at work."

"So, what happened?" Jasper chuckled hearing the annoyance in my tone.

"I got drunk, you weren't there," I responded dryly. "Look, I have to go."

"Okay, Mora. Can we do dinner Monday?"

"I'll check my diary and get back to you." Hanging up, I put my phone on silent and placed it back on the bedside table before huddling back beneath the covers. "Sorry about that."

"Mr. Jones wants you to look at a ring?" Darius asked, a bite in his voice.

"Yes. I didn't expect it this soon. I thought he'd wait till New Year's Eve or something equally cheesy like that." I shook my head with a smile. "I can't believe he's finally willing to commit."

"I take it that it is an engagement ring then?" Darius's voice was deep and gravelly.

"Sure is. Now that he's ready to settle down, Jasper wants to marry next summer and start a family soon after."

Darius was doing that finger tapping thing on his sternum again. "And you are happy with his plans."

I rolled to look at Darius. "Of course, I am. He's not young anymore, and he deserves to be happy."

Darius was out of the bed a moment later. He grabbed up his pillow and quilt and stormed out to the living room slamming the sliding doors after him. I was utterly surprised by his reaction. Lying there, I wondered how I'd offended him. Then it clicked. Darius still thought I was with Jasper. He thought the ring was for me.

Sighing, I rolled onto my side. "It's for the best, Mora. This was never going to work."

***

Darius was gone when I woke in the morning. He left a note telling me not to bother with the conference, to go and enjoy Munich. So, I walked around the city exploring buildings older than the country I was raised in.

In the late morning, I ran into a group of four Australians who were doing the tourist thing and looking for the Hofbräuhaus. It was located immediately across the way from my hotel, so I offered to show them how to find it. In return, they asked me to join them for lunch.

This resulted in a lot of beer drinking on their part and the enjoyment of good German food by all of us. We were still there when dinner came around. Zane, a twenty-five-year-old travel agent who dragged his friends along for a European adventure, planted himself next to me at lunch and hadn't moved.

I wasn't drinking. I wasn't stupid enough to do that with strangers. But I was the only one in the group who wasn't. Just before seven, I watched Darius walk in with some of the people from the conference. They sat at a table across the hall from our corner seat. When Zane's hand found my leg and started sliding up under the hem of my skirt, I took that as my cue to leave.

Bidding everyone farewell, I was halfway to the door when Zane called out. "Come on, Mora. Stay a little longer."

Up until that point, Darius hadn't spotted me. Since I was watching his group as I left, I saw his head snap around at the sound of my name being sung across the hall. Looking back to the group I'd left, I gave them a smile and waved again before continuing out of the hall. I didn't look back at Darius, or acknowledge him. Just took myself back to our room, showered and climbed into bed early.

I vaguely heard Darius come in. He showered, and yet again, I watched him watch me from the doorway to the wardrobe. Eventually, he collected the quilt and pillow and went to the lounge. Again, I went the entire day without seeing him. I was sitting with all our gear packed in the room at five o'clock when the conference ended.

Darius arrived twenty minutes later. "I will pack and then we can get to the airport." I pointed to his bag by the door. "Thank you. Let's go."

The ride to the airport was stone silent. This time, when Tracey offered her services after take-off, Darius accepted. They moved down to the massage bed behind me, she rubbed him down, and then sucked him off.

Retrieving a book I was reading out of my bag, I lost myself in the pages, paying no attention to what was happening directly behind me.

"Miss Ellis?"

Blinking, I realised Tracey was standing looking at me with worry. A quick glance revealed the plane was on the ground. "When did we land?"

Tracey looked amused. "Ten minutes ago. Mr. Rafal wants to know if you plan on joining him in the car or are you catching a taxi?"

"Oh." I unclicked my sash belt and pulled my boots on. "Tell him to go ahead. I can catch the train."

"At eleven at night?" Tracey looked worried. She looked me up and down then looked over her shoulder. "Margaret, tell Mr. Rafal, Miss Ellis will be there in a minute."

The other hostess smiled and stepped out of the plane door.

Tracey sat down as I shoved my book in my bag. "Want to tell me what happened in Munich?"

"Nothing." I stood.

Tracey grabbed my arm and pulled me back into the seat. "Nothing my ass. You are into him, he is into you. Why are you both fucking around with this?"

"Look, I appreciate you're his friend, but you know what he's like. He doesn't date, doesn't have serious relationships. I don't want to be the boss's sex toy. I'm good at my job and I don't want anyone thinking I only got my job because I give good head."

"So quit," Tracey answered with a shrug, as if it was so easy.

"I tried to find another job. They blocked it and refused to release me from my contract," I huffed. "The truth is, most of the time, I love working for him. Working and living with the brothers has been one of the best experiences in my life. It's only when Mr. Rafal and I are left alone it becomes a strain for both of us. If I could just avoid being alone with him, this would be the best job."

Tracey closed her eyes as if in pain. "When you came for me..." She paused and looked away.

"What about it?" I asked totally thrown by the change in subject.

Tracey looked me in the eye. "It was not my fingers you came on."

Confused, I peered at her unsure what to think, then my mind flashed back to her sucking Darius's fingers afterwards. Pure anger flooded my system.

Tracey looked panicked. "Look, it was obvious you were into each other. I know Dare. He was rock hard for you and he turned me down. He's not the sort of guy to do that if it's not real. He didn't want your view of him to be obscured by me.

"Then coming home, he not only took my offer, he pointedly moved us closer to you. I have never massaged him before. He has a masseuse for that in London. I suck his cock when he's horny and that's it. What happened coming home was to goad you. Except, it didn't work. You just put a wall up and, I don't know, you left reality."

Tracey stood and moved out of my way. "You two need to work this out or you will break each other denying what you really want. That's all I'm saying."

Acknowledging she was right didn't simmer my indignation as I stood. "Thank you, Tracey." I held out my hand. She seemed surprised but shook it. "It was nice meeting you."

"You are not angry I tricked you?"

Releasing a soft humored huff, I shook my head and moved to the door. I couldn't be mad with her. I'm not stupid. I knew at the time those weren't her fingers. In truth, I didn't care. I wanted to climax by someone else's touch after four months of my own. My mind just took the acknowledgement of who it was at the time and threw it out the window.

When I arrived at Darius's car, Clark smiled and opened the door. "Welcome back, Miss Ellis."

"Thank you, Clark. Give us a second, will you?" Clark nodded, his smile vanishing.

Dropping down into the seat, I waited till Clark shut the door. "I never want to be alone with you again," I stated calmly. Darius stopped typing into his phone. "If you have to travel, both Warren and I go, or Warren goes with you. Never just us. We fuck up a good working relationship whenever we are left alone. It's stupid that as two grown adults we need to be chaperoned to ensure we behave ourselves, but apparently that's the case."

"Anything else?" Darius growled

Moving toward him, turning my body to half face him getting in his personal space, I kept my tone even, my voice low to ensure it didn't travel out of the car. "You ever fuck me again without my consent, with any part of your body, I'll charge you with rape."

Darius met my eyes surprised. He slowly closed his eyes. "Tracey," he muttered angrily.

Knocking on the window to let Clark know we were done, I sat back in my seat, preventing Darius from saying anything else that he wasn't willing to be overheard.

He was right to be angry with Tracey. She was his friend and his employee; she shouldn't have told me. I liked her better that she did, and I know she told me to try and make me realize that my body reacts to Darius. The fact is, I was already very aware of the effect Darius Rafal had on me.

The problem wasn't that my body lusted for him, or that my heart beat faster in his presence. It was that this was not the sort of man to want marriage and children. I was not going to break my heart on Darius Rafal.

About the Author

Ebony lives in Sydney, Australia, with her husband, daughter, and six cats. She loves to read fantasy, thrillers, and paranormal romance, spending most of her free time with her nose in a book or writing.

Having always possessed an over-active imagination she spent her younger years regaling friends with fantastic stories, holding her audience captive with the passion and suspense of her characters plights.

Now in adulthood she has numerous published works and shows no signs of stopping her imagination from spreading across as many pages as it can find.

If you'd like to follow Ebony or say hi you can find her here:

Facebook: www.facebook.com/EbonyOlson.Author/

Twitter: @Ebony_Olson

Website: http://ebonyolson.com/